Suddenly, the afternoon air felt thick, hot, and pulsating inside him, and he knew he would have to have this girl, too —

"It is the book reviewer's constant hope and occasional reward that once in a while a book such as this will come his way — a story that hits him with the impact of a ton of crushed rock."   — *Houston Chronicle*

Complete and Unabridged

ROOM
for a
STRANGER

(Original title: *The Holiday*)

by

Constantine Fitz Gibbon

WILDSIDE PRESS

Room for a Stranger
(The Holiday)

Published by Wildside Press LLC
www.wildsidepress.com

ROOM
for a
STRANGER

PART I

Chapter One

DR. CHARLES WARREN had finished tying his bow tie, but he went on staring at his face in the mirror. It was pale, faintly puffy, and he disliked it. That heavy jowl, which he noticed in his contemporaries and which he thought of as the New York jowl, that whiteness about the dark eyes, the receding hairline.

"Aren't you ready yet, Charles?"

It was his wife's voice from the next room, her room. He did not answer. Forty-two, he thought, money in the bank, an established career, a pretty wife, two fine children. He moved a little closer to the mirror. Look at the successful diagnostician diagnosing. It was really the humiliation that was so intolerable. At the Jackson's dinner party tonight he would pretend that he had no idea Betty went to bed with Phil Jackson in the afternoons, and so would Phil's wife and so would Betty and only Phil would look oily and pleased and utterly in charge of the situation.

"For God's sake, Charles, what are you doing in there? It's half past seven."

Nasty word, cuckold, nasty thing to be, too. He squared his shoulders and moved away from the glass. Well, if he didn't like it, why didn't he do something about it? Why was he going to dinner with these people? Why

7

wasn't he out getting drunk with the boys? Isn't that what deceived husbands are supposed to do? Or go whoring. Unfortunately he didn't know any boys, only men of his own age and approximately his own income, with wives not unlike his own wife; as for whores, he didn't feel he could start that sort of thing at his age. Besides, he was too tired. Tired all the time, sleeping badly, getting snappy with his children, occasionally questioning his own abilities as a doctor. Just like a character in those advertisements, he thought with a grimace, though he doubted if a change of breakfast food or a patented bedtime drink would do him much good. So why not divorce her? And give her the custody of the children? Oh, no. No, no.

"Charles, what *are* you doing? We're twenty minutes late already."

"All right, all right."

Outside, the March wind blew its vile snow flurries around every New York corner. Inside, the fire of electric logs glowed sullenly, and MacIntyre was talking.

". . . so it seems that when he'd got his Picasso home and hung it upside down, Sue suddenly noticed . . ."

Charles had heard MacIntyre tell this story before. He had even repeated it himself. Perhaps it was new to Jackson. Charles stopped listening. He thought of Picasso's Blue Boy, the sad, southern figure against the sandy background, and then, quite clearly, he remembered the beach at Siano.

It had been during the typhus scare in Naples, when he was a captain in the medical corps, working ten hours a day dusting the beautiful and the deformed, the ponderous and the flighty, the heroes and the cowards, dusting away the epidemic. And then he had had a day off

8

and had got into his jeep and driven south. There were no soldiers in Siano that day, and no lice-infested Neapolitans, and no distant gunfire, but just the grayish-reddish beach that stretched in a semicircle between the cliffs, and the houses piled up above it with, in the middle, the green-tiled dome of the church, and the little café at which he had had his lunch while the exhaustion and the stench of Naples were smoothed away by the gentle breeze from the Tyrrhenian Sea. He rubbed his hand across his eyes. MacIntyre had finished his anecdote and they were all laughing now. He laughed too.

They had reached Seventy-eighth Street and were turning off before he spoke. He said:

"I'm sorry I surprised you kissing Phil Jackson in his library—"

"For heaven's sake, Charles, don't be so silly. I wasn't kissing him."

"Let's not argue about that. At least you'll agree I didn't make a scene. And I shan't make one now. I simply wanted to tell you I'm going away."

"What do you mean?" There was wariness in her voice.

He had drawn up in front of their apartment house. Usually he let her off here and drove on around the corner by himself to the underground garage. He did not switch the engine off; he lit a cigarette, and said:

"I don't particularly want to divorce you—"

"That's mighty handsome of you."

"Principally because of the children. You're a good mother, and I don't want to marry anybody else. So I'm just going to go away for a few months."

Her voice was cold and haughty.

"And where are you going, if it is not presumptuous of your wife to inquire?"

"To Italy. To a place called Siano. I was there once during the war. I feel I need a break and deserve a holiday."

"I see. And what do you suggest that your wife and children, to whom you are so devoted, live on while you're amusing yourself in Italy?"

"Oh for God's sake, Betty. We've plenty of money. Jim can look after the practice while I'm gone. I won't be spending much. Anyhow, you can go and stay with your mother and take the children."

"Thank you. What a lovely suggestion."

He turned now toward her in half light.

"Don't you see," he said, "that I've got to get away and think for a bit?"

"You're the diagnostician. If you're set on loafing, I don't suppose there's much I can say to stop you."

He felt the anger that he had been controlling rising within him. He said:

"There's one thing I'm not set on. I'm not going to stay here till my nerves are so frayed I'll do anything to end this marriage. I'm not going to be bullied into giving you a large alimony, the children, and all those other nice presents you've been day-dreaming about." He pulled himself together, and went on more calmly. "I've got about twenty thousand dollars in the bank. I'll take five of them. You can have the other fifteen. When I come back in six months or so, I'll earn some more. Is that fair?"

She did not answer. He said:

"And now you'd better get out. I want to put the car away and go to bed."

Chapter Two

THE SIANO ROAD TURNED and twisted in a series of sharp loops along the cliff edge. It was a tremendous and deliberately spectacular piece of engineering. Then it dived into a tunnel a half mile long, and that was the end of it. Beyond the tunnel the road became only a few hundred yards of sandy track. For at this point Mussolini's engineers had been needed in Cyrenaica or Abyssinia or Rhodes. Before 1938 it had only been possible to reach Siano by water, or after a lengthy scramble along goat tracks. Now it was almost accessible by car; the road petered out exactly four hundred and twenty-seven stone steps above the piazza.

Charles Warren looked eagerly out of the window of the small, square, green Neapolitan taxi as it emerged from the tunnel. He pushed his briefcase off his knees, onto the seat beside him, and leaned forward. It was exactly as he remembered it to have been, the steep cluster of perhaps forty houses, gray stone or washed plaster, the curve of the beach with the fishing boats pulled up on the sand, the brilliant dome of the baroque church rising like a hen among its chickens. The taxi ground to a halt at the top of the long flight of steps, and Charles jumped out.

"*E bello!*" he said to the driver, who was unloading his two suitcases, his box of paints and his bundle of

11

canvases from the front seat. It was almost his only Italian phrase.

The Neapolitan, a wizened and grimy man beneath his peaked cap, looked up at Charles and smiled. The American had agreed to pay ten thousand lire for the trip, a good price. The Neapolitan still smiled as he carried the bags across to the topmost step. Charles was standing by the wall, looking down, the April sunshine heavy on his dark city suit, his face pale in the heat. Soon he would be in that green-blue ocean, soon he would be soaked in sun. The taxi driver cleared his throat, and Charles took out his pocketbook. He added a thousand-lire tip, though he knew this was not necessary, and turned back to drink his fill of the rolling blue hills that reared up at either end of the beach.

"Grazie, signore!"

He did not look about as he heard the taxi turn and start to rattle away. There was no other sound save for a faint humming of bees and then, down below, the great bell of the church that began slowly to toll. This was his dream: this was perfect.

In answer to an unuttered wish a boy had appeared, a bronzed and barefoot boy of fifteen or so, in faded blue trousers that reached halfway down his calves and a faded khaki shirt open to the waist. He said something that Charles could not understand, then pointed at the bags, his teeth very white in his smiling face. Charles nodded. The boy picked up the two cases, the paints and the canvases, and Charles looked around for his briefcase.

The tunnel was empty, the little semicircle of light at the far end unobstructed. Oh well, it was not really so serious. Almost all his money was in the briefcase, but luckily he had had it changed into traveler's checks which were valueless without his signature and which he could

12

reclaim from the Transatlantic Express Company. There were a few papers and letters, nothing important, and his passport. That would have to be reported. It was a nuisance, but it did not really spoil his mood as he followed the boy down those many steps. In a few weeks, he thought, the backs of his knees would no longer ache at the climb. His body would be as healthy and strong as it used to be. He would paint a little, if he felt like it, swim, drink the clear, cold white wine at the café on the beach, learn enough Italian to play cards with the fishermen, maybe go out occasionally with the fishing fleet at night. Yesterday evening, in the dirt and noise and confusion of Naples, he had wondered if he had been mistaken in coming here. Now he was sure he had done right.

They passed through the piazza. The big church with its steps filled one side. Facing it were the post office and the *Municipio,* outside which there lounged a young policeman in the brown uniform of the carabinieri. Lazy shops without customers lined the other two walls. This was the middle of the afternoon. The Sianesi, he realized, would all be taking their siestas at this hour, as he would be doing himself tomorrow. He felt hot in his dark suit, with his raincoat over his arm, and did not notice the two women in black dresses who were peering at him, their faces closed despite their curiosity, from the back of the shop that sold hardware.

The hundred or so steps from the piazza down to the beach were older, steeper, worn down in the middle. The houses here were all of flaking gray stone, with unpainted shutters. On the left, behind a four-foot wall, was the graveyard attached to the church, and then the staircase became a narrow, twisting passage between the houses. Occasionally a birdcage was hung outside a window, but no bird sang. Perhaps the cages were empty. Suddenly they were on the beach.

The café jutted farther forward than the dozen or so other houses that lined the beach. Downstairs there was an open, roofed terrace with a few tables; above it was a veranda on which stood plants in pots, creeping plants the name of which Charles did not know, but which gave a pretty, almost festive appearance to the little balcony. The entrance to the café was from the beach side, across the small terrace. In front of the doorway there hung a sort of string curtaining, lengths of cord about which had been bent innumerable metal bottle tops. They rattled together as the boy pushed his way through into the dark interior. Charles followed and for a moment could see nothing in the cool darkness. Then he made out a stout, middle-aged man with heavy mustaches leaning his elbows on a counter at the far end. There were three or four tables in here too, and advertisements for vermouth, and a holy picture, and a calendar. Otherwise the room was bare and the floor was stone.

Charles had preserved a perfectly clear picture of the place as it had been on the occasion of his only visit, nearly ten years ago. Nothing had changed except, presumably, the calendar. Only then the place had been owned by a woman with a small daughter. She had been able to speak some English. Foolishly, perhaps, it had never occurred to him that she might not be here now, for his memory had been utterly static, as was the place itself, and since Siano had not changed through the last two or three centuries, so he had assumed that the amiable woman would be in the café and the little girl would wait at table. Now he said:

"Do you speak English?"

"Sure," said the man, talking somewhat out of the

14

corner of his mouth. He came around from behind the bar.

Charles told him of his previous visit—"That was my wife," the man put in—and explained that he was planning to stay for some little time. The man had been watching him carefully. He said:

"This ain't the season. You can't stay here. You can live at Maria's and eat here. O.K.?"

It sounded all right. The proprietor of the café walked down to Maria's with him. It was a single, large room, right on the beach, with its own lavatory, simply furnished but comfortable. Old Maria would keep it clean. It seemed just what he wanted. The price, too, was fair, and the charge for meals at the café very reasonable. The whole business was completed in five minutes. It was only when this had been done that the man's face became friendly and smiling.

"You wanna come back and have a drink with me?"

As they walked along the beach Charles asked after his wife.

"Dead," said the man.

Charles was about to say something, when the man went on.

"Adelmo is my name. What's yours?"

Charles told him, and congratulated him on his knowledge of English.

"I was in New York for six years."

"Was that why I didn't see you when I was here before?"

"When you was here before I was a prisoner, over in Africa. I was in New York twenty-eight to thirty-four." They had pushed through the bottle-top curtain. Adelmo gave some orders to the boy who had carried the bags and told Charles to tip him two hundred lire. The boy

15

went and Adelmo said: "What you want? Whisky? Wine?"

"I'd like a bottle of wine if you'll share it with me."

"Sure."

And he fetched, from somewhere at the back, a bottle without a label, beaded with cold. The sides of the coarse tumblers clouded at once. Just such a bottle did Charles remember. It was delicious, and the sweat dried on him as he sipped it in this cool, dark bar.

"You like something to eat?"

Charles was hungry, and once again Adelmo disappeared through the door behind his bar. He was wearing an old pair of American army trousers, a dark flannel shirt without a collar, and a dark, unbuttoned waistcoat. Charles heard him call:

"Concetta!" and then say something in Italian which he did not understand. When Adelmo had returned to the table, Charles told him about his stupidity in leaving the briefcase in the taxi. At once Adelmo's unshaven face assumed an expression of gravity, almost of anger.

"Naples bastards!" he said, briefly.

"It was my fault, really."

"You got the taxi number?"

"No, I . . ."

"We go and see my brother. He's the *sindaco* here, the boss, the mayor. After you eat your spinach I take you see my brother. He'll fix that Naples bastard."

The girl who now entered the bar from the back was tall and slender and extraordinarily graceful. The Greeks had been in these parts, and after them the Arabs had raided along this coast for a thousand years. Perhaps it was from some mixture of those bloods that she had inherited her aquiline and yet warm features, her figure that was full without a trace of coarseness, her huge black

16

eyes and her ivory complexion. She placed a dish of ham, some olives, bread and butter before Charles. He looked up at her, smiled and said thank you. She nodded without smiling and turned away. His eyes followed her in her cotton dress as she moved away, back through the door behind the bar. He said to Adelmo,

"Is she your daughter?"

"Yes. Concetta is my daughter. You like olives?"

"Very much." He buttered a portion of bread and took a mouthful of the ham. "You've a beautiful daughter. I remember her when I was here before. She was just a little thing."

"Yes? Concetta is a good girl, a good cook. You want another glass of wine?"

She had re-entered the bar, carrying a plate on which were cheese and an orange. Charles said:

"Does Concetta speak English?"

It was she who answered, slowly:

"A little."

"You don't remember me, but I was here before once, when you were a little girl."

She did not smile.

"I remember you. You were a capitano in the American army. You had lunch, out on the terrace."

Charles Warren was flattered. He was about to speak, when Adelmo said something quickly to his daughter. She turned away immediately and disappeared through the back. Adelmo said:

"You wanna eat your cheese? Then we go see my brother."

Charles was about to reply but thought better of it. He finished his cheese. The orange he would leave. As they emerged through the metallic curtain into the sunshine, Adelmo said, almost apologetically:

17

"Concetta she gotta make the soup now, *zuppa di pesce,* fish soup, like a fish chowder back in the States. These girls, they talk all day and do no work if you let them. But Concetta's a good girl."

They made their way together up the steep steps.

The mayor's office was a small, untidy room with a picture of a bearded man hanging crooked on the wall behind the mayor's chair. Adelmo's brother was fatter and greasier than the publican and exuded an air of self-importance as he sat back in his overstuffed armchair, twiddling his thumbs. After the introductions had been performed, Charles was politely forced into an equally overstuffed, pink chair opposite the mayor's desk. Adelmo remained standing, leaning against the window that overlooked the piazza. The two brothers carried on a brief conversation in Italian. Then Adelmo said to Charles:

"My brother the mayor asks what was in your suitcase?"

"Briefcase. Tell him it contained four thousand dollars . . . in traveler's checks . . . and a few personal papers, including my passport."

Adelmo raised his eyebrows at the sum of money, and then rapidly translated for the mayor's benefit. They both talked at the same time, or so it seemed to Charles, and then Adelmo said:

"My brother he says this is very serious. So much money. He says we must go at once to the cops. . . ."

The mayor had heaved himself out of his chair, buttoned his coat and, after grimacing his apologies, preceded Adelmo and Charles down the stairs. The police lived on the ground floor. There were two of them, the member of the carabinieri whom Charles had seen on arrival and another, slightly older man, the *maresciallo.* It was the latter who did the talking for the police and

18

he, the mayor and Adelmo carried on a fairly lengthy conversation, of which Charles was obviously the subject. This made him feel faintly embarrassed, as though he were somehow on show. He ran his fingers along the top of the big, old-fashioned typewriter that stood on the *maresciallo's* desk. Suddenly the *maresciallo* turned toward him, bowed, and spoke rapidly for several minutes. Charles guiltily took his hand away from the typewriter. He was feeling more and more foolish. At last the policeman had finished and Adelmo translated while the mayor and the *maresciallo* with folded arms and smiles creasing their fat faces, watched approvingly. The other, younger policeman gazed impassively at the scene.

"He say you not to worry. He ring through to Naples police at once. The Italian police very good and quick. You have your case back at once, maybe tonight. Now you must fill in the papers, the *permesso di sogiorno* and he must see your passport."

It was explained about the passport. The papers were produced, which Adelmo helped Charles fill in. The *maresciallo* read them through and frowned. Then they all shook hands and the two policemen saluted, with more vigor than smartness. As they were walking back across the piazza, where there were now one or two people about who watched them curiously, Charles thanked Adelmo for the trouble he had taken on his behalf. Adelmo said, simply:

"Here we are friends. We help each other. That's right, eh?" And then, changing his tone: "Don't you worry. They'll get your case. The Naples cops very smart."

"I hope so. Not that it matters so much. If I haven't got it back in three or four days, I'll just have the checks canceled."

"You have it back before that. You no need worry."

19

They had crossed the piazza now, and were descending the steps. In a corner, by the low wall of the churchyard, there sat a little boy of three or four, sobbing bitterly. Adelmo stopped and asked him something. Through his tears the child answered, and Adelmo, making consoling noises, patted him on the head. Charles asked:

"What's the matter with him? Has he hurt himself?"

Adelmo bent over him and asked him another question. The boy, his sobs quenched by his curiosity as he gazed at the stranger through very round eyes, gave a distracted answer. Adelmo straightened up:

"Luigi says the other kids they took his ball and threw it over the wall here. Then they run away."

"Poor little fellow," said Charles. And then, after a moment's hesitation, he vaulted the wall. He landed on the green mound of a grave. All around him were tombs, some with ornate white statuary, most marked only with a simple stone. At the far end of the churchyard, by the church, an elderly priest was walking up and down reading his breviary. He looked up at Charles, but the American was too far away to see the man's expression. The ball was close by his feet, a large, red one. He tossed it over the wall, waved in what he hoped was an explanatory and also apologetic gesture toward the priest, and vaulted back into the lane of steps. The ball was bouncing away down to the beach, the child scrambling after it. Charles was slightly out of breath and smiling somewhat fatuously. Adelmo said:

"You like kids?"

"Yes, very much."

"You not married?"

Charles had got his breath back and he frowned. He said:

"No." And then, after a pause: "No, I'm not."

At the café he left Adelmo, and made his way along the beach to what was his new home. Two fishermen, one young and one old, were fixing their nets that lay stretched out upon the sand. The sun was sinking toward the west.

"*Buona sera!*" Charles called out, as he passed by the fishermen They straightened, looked at him, and after a moment the elder one said:

"*Buona sera, signore!*"

Charles walked on, wondering whether or not to go for a swim. He decided he would. He did not know that the two fishermen had not immediately returned to their work. They were watching him. And up on the balcony of the café an old man, Adelmo's father, sat in his chair and watched, too. He could not see very well, and he was most curious to know about the foreigner's appearance. He reached for the binoculars that an American soldier had once lost here. He lifted them to his eyes and thus he had a good look at Charles's back as he disappeared into Maria's. Then he put down the binoculars. There was nothing else for him to look at on the beach.

Chapter Three

EACH DAY THE SUN GREW HOTTER, and the blue-green hills up above Siano were becoming tinged with brown. At midday the sand burned Charles's bare feet; he would wear his rope-soled shoes down to the rippling water's

21

edge, and when he came out of the sea his body, now tanned, would be dry within minutes, almost seconds. A heat haze hung along the horizon. Soon even the Sianesi would be going for a swim.

Charles, in his bathing trunks, with a straw hat on his head, and his painting gear under his arm, walked along the morning beach. He set up his easel and looked at his half-completed canvas. Usually, if it were not a school day, the children would gradually converge about him as he painted, and little Luigi, with his red ball, was always there. He was too young for school. Today, being the feast day of Siano's patron saint, was surely not a school day. Perhaps the children were all in church, for the great bell had been tolling since early morning. He looked about him. There was nobody at all on the beach, or was that someone down there by the boats? He walked toward them.

It was Mario and his father. Mario often came to the café in the evening, a shy and extremely handsome young man. Occasionally Charles had played *scopa* with him and one or two others, banging down the greasy cards that seemed so very foreign with their pictures of horsemen and gold cups and bundles of staves. The men played seriously, had no false pride about their delight in taking each other's money, but also showed their pleasure when, rarely, Charles won. Mario had promised to take Charles out fishing one of these nights. After three weeks in the village Charles could speak a little Italian, enough for *scopa* and for fishing at any rate.

"Heigh, Mario!"

Mario looked up and smiled. He, too, was painting, painting the eye on the prow of his boat that would guide his father and himself to fish and safety through the waters. Mario's father glanced briefly at Charles and went back to his work on the keel. The smell of paint and tar was heavy and somehow exciting. That afternoon, Charles knew, the village priest together with a visiting dignitary of the Church, would bless Siano's little fishing fleet. Mario and his father were working against time. The eye on the front of the boat was very wide open. Charles walked back toward his easel.

Would the postman be coming by today? It was two weeks now since Charles had written to the Express Company about his stolen checks. Each day he had waited for the gaunt, one-eyed figure with the bag slung over his shoulder. There had been an acknowledgement from Naples: they were informing their New York office and he would be hearing from them almost immediately. And each day the postman, tall as a tree and apparently forever locked up in some secret, smiling dream, passed slowly down the beach. Yesterday he had even brought Charles a letter:

"*Ecoolo, signore*," he had said, and with a flourish had produced the envelope. It was from his wife. She was taking the children to her mother's on Long Island. She did think that he might at least have had the common good manners to write her a line. The children were well. They had got his postcards.

Presumably the postman would not be coming today. Perhaps he went to church too, though he hardly looked like a Christian. Maria, he knew, was in church, for she had cleaned his room almost before he was out of bed, and she had been wearing her black dress. He had just reached his easel when the bell began to ring again. It was not the big one, and it was being rung at a great rate. Simultaneously he saw a handful of people emerge onto the beach, at the foot of the stairs, and disperse.

Charles painted for a few minutes, but his heart was

not in it today. There was an atmosphere of suppressed excitement in the village which reached down even to the beach. Two or three men, he could see, were seated on the terrace in front of Adelmo's café, which was unusual at this time of day, and once, across the sand, he heard a distant burst of laughter. He put away his paints and began to walk toward them.

He was still a hundred yards or so away when he saw Concetta come out of the café. She was wearing a loose beach wrap of white toweling, and the men must have spoken to her, for she stopped on the terrace. Then Charles heard the men laugh again and she walked on, down toward the water. Charles changed his direction, so that he would meet her by the edge, but she was there ahead of him.

She had taken off her wrap—she was wearing a white bathing suit, which struck him as surprisingly sophisticated for this little village—and was sitting down, untying her shoes. When his shadow fell across her, she looked up. He wished her a good morning and she replied, although without any evident pleasure or emotion. They did not know one another at all well, even though she had brought him his meals in the café for these past three weeks. Whenever he had attempted to engage her in conversation she had replied, politely but usually in monosyllables, and then gone back to whatever she did out of sight in the rear of the house. Sometimes, he had noticed, she did stop to talk to one of the fishermen for a few minutes, usually Mario, but Charles had not really tried to get to know her. For one thing, there was the language barrier; for another, in the café, he would be sitting and she standing, and this had made him feel awkward when talking to her. Now he said, somewhat fatuously:

24

"Are you going for a swim?"

"Oh yes," and she began to push her long, curly black hair into the white bathing cap.

"May I come with you?"

"Of course."

She got up and waited politely while he kicked off his shoes. Then they walked into the water side by side.

"It's cold!" she said and laughed.

It seemed almost tepid to Charles. The Atlantic was never so warm as this, even in August. The sea was absolutely smooth, yet still it managed to produce a solitary, half-hearted wave, which was nearer a ripple, as it reached the shore. They waded through this, and the pebbly sand beneath their feet shelved rapidly away.

"Go on," he said, and smiled at her.

She smiled back.

"No, you go."

He dived into the water and swam half a dozen strokes out to sea. Then he turned on his back and looked toward the beach. He could see her white cap. He thought of swimming in toward her, but decided against it and headed for deeper water. When he stepped out at last onto the beach, dripping, short of breath and invigorated with the salt and the coolness, she was lying down on her wrap, her hair loose about her shoulders once again. He sat down beside her, took a pack of Chesterfields and a lighter from inside the shoe where he had left them, and offered her one.

"No, thank you. I do not smoke."

He took a deep puff. He was almost dry already. She had closed her eyes again and was lying on her back, her ankles crossed, her arms straight down by her sides. Yet it was not as though she wished him to go away. He looked around the beach. Mario and his father had left their boat and were walking toward the café. As they passed, twenty yards higher up, Charles saw that they were both looking at him. He raised his hand in a gesture that was not quite a wave, but neither Mario nor his father answered. He said to the girl:

"What time is the procession?"

"At three o'clock, up in the piazza."

She opened her eyes now and looked up at him.

"Can I go with you to see it?"

"Of course. Everybody goes to see it."

He was not sure if she had understood his question. It was very hot.

"I—" he began, but from up by the café came Adelmo's voice.

"Con-*cett*-a! Con-*cett*-a!"

She sat up at once and sighed. Adelmo was standing on the edge of his terrace. Concetta got to her feet, slipped her toes into her sandals, and put on her wrap. She was about to walk away, when Charles said:

"Wait for me, I'll come with you."

Obediently she did so, and they started across the beach together. Up on the café balcony he saw the old man, and for a second the sun glinted on the glass of his binoculars. He said:

"He's your grandfather, isn't he?"

"Yes, my grandfather."

"I've never seen him downstairs."

"He has not been down for five years. He is happy up there with his *binocoli*." It was the longest sentence that she had ever spoken to him.

He said with a tone of amusement:

"What does he look at?"

"He watches what's happening," she replied.

26

"But nothing ever does happen here. . . ."

She replied:

"Well, this morning there was us . . ." He glanced down at her quickly, but her tone was calm and natural, nor did she look up at him. After a moment's pause she went on:

". . . and later he'll watch the *festa,* when the priests come down to bless the boats."

They had reached the café terrace. Adelmo spoke to her rapidly in an Italian which Charles could not understand. Adelmo looked worried and hot in his best clothes and he kept mopping his brow with a big, red cotton handkerchief. She disappeared into the building, and Charles was about to sit down at one of the tables, when Adelmo turned to him and said:

"Can I speak with you, *signore,* please?"

"Why of course."

But apparently Adelmo did not wish to talk there, on the terrace, beneath the eyes of the men, and Charles followed him down onto the beach.

"What is it, Adelmo?"

"Maria she spoke to me after we leave the church. She is worried about her money. Maria is a poor woman and it's three weeks now . . ."

Charles felt transitory annoyance. He did not like being taken aside in this way, as though what had to be discussed were somehow discreditable. He said:

"But Adelmo, you know I'm waiting for my checks to be cleared. I haven't got any money until that's done. I explained it all to Maria as best I could. Didn't you tell her?"

"Sure I tell her, but she's a dumb peasant woman. She don't understand about checks and that. She understood your money been stolen. She wonder why you don't get some more."

"But I am getting some more, that's exactly what I'm doing."

"O.K., *signore*, but Maria is worried."

"Well tell her I'll write to the Express Company again, tomorrow, when the post office is open. I don't see what more I can do."

"O.K., I tell her that."

Charles was not really put out by this short conversation. He knew that these people had been extraordinarily good to him, letting him live here almost without money —for he had had only the equivalent of twenty dollars in his pocketbook when he arrived—and Adelmo had been particularly friendly and helpful. But he really did not see what he, or they, could do except wait for the Express Company to clear his checks. It could not, he was sure, be long now.

As he and Adelmo climbed the few wooden steps that led to the terrace, he said:

"What were you doing in New York in the twenties, Adelmo?"

"Bootlegger. Me and my boss, we make moonshine, thousands and thousands of gallons of moonshine. Then prohibition finish and my boss he say to me: 'We all washed up here in New York, Adelmo. Here's a couple thousand bucks. You beat it back home.' So I come back home."

Both men laughed. Adelmo said:

"You like me fix you a nice bottle moonshine one day? Make you drunk as a skunk."

"Thanks, but I think I'll stick to your wine. In fact I'll have a bottle now."

"O.K., I get you a good one and put it down on your account."

Charles looked around for Mario, but he had gone. He did not know the three men who were seated on the terrace, so he drank his wine alone. It was Adelmo who brought him out his lunch a little later, shrimps and an omelette and melon and cheese. The big church bell was ringing again.

Charles had not realized that so many people lived in and about Siano. The steps leading to the piazza were bedecked with arches which were laden with flowers and strung with lines of colored electric light bulbs, now unlit. There were tables and chairs before some of the houses, and in the corners of the piazza were booths, rickety and crudely painted. The little square was crowded, the men in their dark clothes walking about, the women standing in knots by the doorways, and children dodging between the legs of the grown-ups. There was a heavy hum of conversation in the air.

Charles, being taller than most of the people in the square, could see over their heads as soon as he reached the top of the steps. It had amused him to put on his best gray-flannel suit for the occasion, and he was glad that he had done so. Even the two carabinieri were wearing comparatively clean white uniforms today and the one-eyed postman had donned a canary yellow, turtle-neck sweater, which must have been very hot in the mid-afternoon sunshine. Charles's eyes traveled over the crowd until, on the far side of the square, opposite the church, he saw Concetta. She was standing alone, her eyes fixed on the great church door, and he began to make his way toward her.

29

"*Buongiorno, signor dottore,*" said the old postman in his dreamy voice, as Charles pushed past him.

"Hello," said Charles, and went on. A small child stared, round-eyed, up into his face, but did not for a moment stop licking the enormous toffee-apple that he clutched in both his sticky hands.

"*Scusi,*" said Charles, "*scusi,*" as he treaded his way between the tables and a group of older, more serious men. They moved politely aside:

"*Prego, dottore.*"

He did not realize that these people all knew him to be a doctor, but then, of course, he had had to write down his profession on the form that the police had given him.

He came up behind Concetta and laid his hand on her arm. She did not seem surprised; perhaps she had seen him coming. She smiled at him and then turned back to face the church doors again. He was about to ask her why she had not waited for him, down at the café, but changed his mind. The bell was tolling incessantly, and at that moment there was an explosion of rockets up on the hill above Siano. The crowd gasped.

"Ah!" said the crowd. "Ah!"

"What's that for?" Charles asked Concetta.

She glanced at him and smiled. He thought she had not understood his question.

"What do the rockets mean?" he repeated, and took her arm again.

"They honor our saint. . . . It is the start of the *festa.*"

And then the church doors opened. The crowd swayed back, to clear a space, and in the sudden crush Charles was nearly separated from Concetta. Only by holding tightly to her could he prevent the people from forcing them apart. He stood his ground, so that by the time the

30

crowd had settled down, he and Concetta were nearly in the front rank of spectators. He did not let go of her arm. All the church bells were ringing now, as fast and as loudly as they could. The procession began to come out from the dark, candle-studded interior.

First to appear were twenty or so young men in dark suits, their expression very solemn and serious. Among them Charles recognized Mario and one or two others whom he had seen in the café. They walked slowly around the piazza, two by two, and in the middle of the group was an older man, carrying a large maroon-colored flag. The crowd watched them in dead silence, broken only by the wailing of a small child. When the head of the column had completed the circuit and reached the top of the steps that led down to the beach, they stopped. At that minute a small brass band, up above and out of sight, struck up a march. Every head in the crowd turned away from the young men and toward the invisible band. Once again there was an audible gasp and a mutter of whispered conversation. The talk stopped when the next group came out of the church.

These were the old people, first a dozen aged men, each carrying a lighted candle. Thump, thump, thump went the band, and one by one the candles gutted and went out as the old men made the circle of the square. The younger ones in front had meanwhile begun to go down the stairs. Next came a group of old women, all in black with black veils. They could not complete their tour of the piazza, for the old men were blocking the way, and they stopped opposite Charles and Concetta. At that moment the band ceased playing.

Charles whispered:

"Why has the band stopped?"

"It started too soon."

31

Charles laughed and then was conscious that the old women were staring at Concetta and himself. He asked, in a low voice:

"Who are the old ladies?"

"The widows . . ."

I bet they're terrible old gossips, he thought, but he did not let go of Concetta's arm. There was another salvo from up on the hill and the procession moved off once again. Now from the church came two files of thirteen-year-old girls, dressed in white with blue veils. Some kept their eyes fixed slightly above the heads of the crowd, an expression of piety on their faces, but others, naughtier girls, glanced about them, their black eyes very bright despite the veils.

"Did you used to walk with them?" he asked Concetta.

"Sh . . . !" she whispered.

Next there was a group of little boys, also marching two by two. They wore white and scarlet, save for two who had on monk's brown habits. Charles recognized little Luigi at the same moment that Luigi saw him. The child made as though to run across to him, but a slightly older boy, walking behind, gave him a pinch. For a second or two Luigi's face was wrinkled, so that Charles feared he was going to burst into tears. However, he pulled himself together and went on, very upright and manly.

Charles had not realized that the bells had ceased pealing, and only now, as the big one began again, did he notice how amazingly silent the piazza had been. Yet the excitement of the crowd was increasing, almost tangible through his hand that held Concetta's arm. To the booming of the bell was now added another sound, for a group of very little girls, dressed all in white, had passed out under the great, elaborate doorway, singing as they

32

came. At first they were nervous and their voices barely audible, but when the bell stopped once again they could be clearly heard. They sang most sweetly. And then the bell tolled, one, two and three, and the little girls fell silent. The statue of the saint was being borne out of the church; a great sigh passed through the crowd.

The statue was a bust, double life-size, and rested on an ornate glass-and-gilt base which contained relics. It was very brightly painted, the lips and cheeks crimson, the eyes of forget-me-not blue, the hair brown. Charles thought that it looked extraordinarily ugly, with the foolish simper of beatitude on its face, but he realized that he alone had such a reaction to the painted idol. It was carried by four men in dark suits. They were already red in the face, and the statue was obviously both heavy and awkward. The bell had stopped. For a moment they stood upon the topmost step and then, up on the hill, came the explosion of rockets, and they set off, the men lurching a little, the statue jerking above the heads of the crowd in pace with their unsteady gait.

Behind the statue, in crimson and lace, came the priests, two in front, then the mitred bishop with a canopy that four little acolytes held above him, then two more. The priests were chanting and the bishop scattered his blessings to right and to left. But they had hardly emerged full into the piazza before their chanting was drowned by the band that had struck up again. And at the same time all the people began to throw handfuls of petals at the statue of their patron saint. The competition from the band was too much for the priests, or perhaps they had finished their chant. In any case they stopped, and part of the deluge of petals aimed at the saint fluttered down upon their beautiful and elaborate vestments.

Concetta was taking handfuls from a pocket in her

33

skirt and throwing them in the curious, ungainly way of girls. The procession was moving very slowly around the square amidst considerable, though subdued, noise from the people. Suddenly Concetta turned to Charles and thrust some petals into his right hand. Her expression was open and happy and so gay that he almost kissed her. But she had turned away and was once again tossing the multi-colored petals at the painted statue, which had passed by them now and would soon be beyond her range. For what seemed to Charles a very long time he looked at her full, young profile, the curve of her flushed cheek brushed by the thick black hair. Then he raised his eyes and met those of the village priest.

This was the man whom he had seen when he jumped the graveyard wall, those weeks ago. He had passed him in the piazza on subsequent occasions, but they had never spoken. Now the priest was looking right at him gravely from hard, black eyes in an old, chalky face. Had those thin lips beneath the beaked nose ever smiled? They were not smiling now. He looked straight into Charles's eyes, and Charles felt a sudden cold despite the great heat of the day. And then Charles looked away.

At this moment a small boy, on the far side of the piazza, hurled his petals at the statue. He had held them so tightly in his sticky hand—for it was the boy who had been eating the toffee-apple—that they had formed an almost solid ball. It curved through the air, missed the saint by a good six feet, and burst in painless and brilliant shrapnel against Charles's forehead. The people immediately about Charles burst out laughing, and so did he. Concetta turned, and laughing too, brushed the petals from his shoulders. He had dropped his own handful to the ground. In any case, it was too late now. The saint would soon be going down the steps to the beach.

34

The priests were followed by a procession of middle-aged men with the mayor at their head, and as a fitting climax there came, crescendo, the six-man band. Blasting and blowing, they had climbed down from the heights. Now they joined in behind the old men. On this occasion there had been no mistake in timing. And the whole crowd jostled after them. Charles took Concetta's arm once again. She was pressed close to his side in the now noisy, cheerful crowd that followed its patron. He took her hand in his and tightened his grip on her fingers. He felt her return his pressure. He glanced down at her and she was looking up into his face.

All the colored lights were lit, and the dome of the church, too, was illuminated, so that the piazza was a crowded elegant fairyland when Charles arrived there at eight o'clock that night. He had had numerous drinks down at Adelmo's and the spectacular beauty of the little square was breathtaking. The booths, too, were lit up, and on the tables stood wine and glasses; for tonight these were impromptu open-air cafés. The band was playing down on the beach now, though he understood that later there would be dancing in the piazza. For a moment Charles stood on the threshold of gaiety. Then he heard a voice:

"Dottore! Dottore!"

It was his new friend, the postman. Standing up by one of the tables, he held a bottle in his hand at which he pointed with unambiguous invitation. Charles made his way across to him.

The postman poured out a tumbler of the red wine, and gave Charles a great slap on the back. It was not only down on the beach that the patron saint's passing had been celebrated with abundance. The postman insisted on Charles taking his chair—all the others were occupied. Indeed he forced him down into it, so that he was sitting extremely close to a very stout lady who sipped and sipped and seemed quite incapable of understanding any remark that Charles made to her. The gaunt postman—Charles noticed that he had spilled a certain amount of red wine down the front of his pullover—stood over them, grinning, urging Charles to drink up the sulphurous and heavy wine, filling his glass as soon as it was half empty. There could really be no conversation in the hubbub, even if they had had any ideas to exchange or any language in which to do so. Charles drank and when the bottle was empty he bought another from the wild-looking girl who seemed to be in charge. The postman grinned down at him and the fat lady sipped away busily. Charles looked around for Concetta.

She had brought him his supper at Adelmo's with her customary demure efficiency, threading her way through the café which was more crowded than ever before. He had managed at last to ask her if she would come up to the piazza with him. She had said, quickly, that she would see him up there, and then had turned away to help her father. He half wondered if she would come, as he drank the strong wine. The postman was banging him on the shoulder. The postman raised his glass.

"Viva America!" he shouted.

Nobody took any notice. The fat lady sipped on.

Charles got to his feet. He tried to raise his glass, but the postman held his wrist and insisted on first filling it to the very brim.

"Viva Italia!" said Charles and drank. He was about to replace his glass on the table, when the postman stopped him. He made it plain, by example, that he expected

Charles to drink the whole glass down. Charles did so. Immediately the postman filled it to the brim again.

"*Viva New York!*" cried the postman. Still no one took any notice of this little scene. Charles did not feel he had to finish his glass this time, but he must propose an equally friendly toast.

"*Viva Napoli!*"

It was not well received.

"*Napoli, bah!*" said the postman, lurching slightly. The fat lady giggled. But the postman's ugly, one-eyed face soon lit up again.

"*Viva Chicago!*" he cried and drained his glass.

Charles began to fear an alcoholic tour of the entire United States. But at that moment he saw Concetta coming into the piazza. The postman apparently saw her, too, for when Charles tried, by dumbshow, to explain that he must be leaving, the postman gave him a great dig in the ribs with his elbow, and with a burst of laughter said something that Charles was glad he could not understand. The fat lady giggled more merrily than ever. Charles and the postman clicked glasses once again, then Charles downed what was left in his and walked across to Concetta. From the beach below came the somewhat distorted strains of *La Bohème*. Charles felt a tingling excitement, a joy of living which would have seemed to him incredible a month ago, in that great city to which he and his new-found friend had just drunk.

Slowly they made the tour of the piazza, stopping at the booths. The first that they came to was a shooting gallery, the targets being dead electric bulbs strung on wires. Charles bought five slugs for himself and five for Concetta. She hit no bulb, but he got one and the tinkle of the glass attracted a handful of spectators.

"Would you like another five?" he asked her. The

proprietor of the booth, who had a fine, curled mustache, had already placed them on the wooden ledge before her.

"No, I can hit nothing. You go again."

He paid, and this time he was more successful, knocking out four of the bulbs. The spectators were impressed and one, an old fisherman whom Charles had frequently seen down at Adelmo's, slapped him on the back, grinning to show his yellowing stumps of teeth. The proprietor of the booth, too, was lavish in his expressions of wonderment at the foreign gentleman's virtuosity; it was the least he could do, for his booth offered no prizes. Charles and Concetta strolled on. She said:

"You are very good with a gun. All Americans shoot a lot, don't they?"

He stopped and looked down at her. Her face was serious.

"What do you mean?"

"In the war, the soldiers that come here for their rest, they used to shoot at things."

"What things?"

"Bottles mostly. Sometimes, when they drunk, they shoot at other things, flowerpots on people's balconies. Once some G.I.'s shoot at the church, how do you call it? The *gallo* on the top that shows the wind."

"The weather cock?"

"Yes."

Charles frowned.

"Soldiers . . ." he began, but he did not go on. There was no point in it. They had reached a stall where an old woman was selling scarves and straw hats and balloons and pocket-knives that had a picture of Vesuvius painted on the ivory handle. He stopped when he saw Concetta looking at a red silk square.

"How much?" he asked the old woman in Italian.

38

"Three thousand lire, signore," she replied and began at once to extol the fine quality of the silk, to explain how well it would suit the signorina's style of beauty. Charles took out his pocketbook. It was almost all the money he had left, but he bought it.

"Oh," said Concetta, when he gave it to her, "it is beautiful, but it is too much. . . . It is . . ."

"Nonsense," said Charles. "It's nothing . . . a souvenir . . . a souvenir of the *festa* . . ."

She held it on her two hands, as though it were a tray, and her expression, as she looked up at him, was serious, almost apprehensive. He began:

"What shall we . . . oh, hello, Mario!"

Mario was standing close beside him, and looked awkward out of his fisherman's clothes. He was wearing the same suit, of a hideous peacock blue, that he had had on during the procession.

"Ullo, signor Carlo," said Mario and then stopped, his eyes on Concetta, who was still holding the scarf before her. It was a moment of immobility. Then Mario spoke rapidly to Concetta in Italian.

"What's he saying?" Charles asked.

But she had answered Mario in her own language and he, too, had spoken again. At last she said to Charles:

"I must go now. Mario . . . he want me to go back down to the café with him."

Mario, slightly flushed, was nodding.

Charles said:

"Oh, what nonsense. The *festa's* hardly begun. Let's have a bottle of wine together, the three of us." There was a table close by, from which three other people had just risen. "Come on, Mario, *una bottiglia de vino . . . si?*"

The girl who sold wine was standing, hands on hips,

waiting. Mario said something in Italian which again Charles could not understand. Concetta translated:

"He say he must go and I with him."

Impatiently Charles turned to the girl and ordered a bottle of the red and three glasses. He pushed Mario down into a chair, as had been done to him an hour or so ago. He filled up the three glasses and raised his to Mario. Now the fisherman gave a tentative smile and they drank. Charles had just raised his to his lips for a second swallow, when he was slapped on the back. Some of the wine splashed on his gray flannel suit. He turned around. It was the postman, by this time in a fairly advanced stage of intoxication, whom Charles had not noticed at the next table.

The postman began at once to tell him some lengthy anecdote or joke, which Charles was quite unable to understand, the more so as the band had now installed itself on the church steps and was playing loudly. The postman bawled, the fat lady, who had acquired a pink balloon, giggled, and Charles strained his ears to catch the sense. At last the postman seemed to have reached the climax of his story and Charles laughed. The postman looked surprised, and Charles wondered if perhaps he had been mistaken, if the story had been a tragic one or even a political disquisiton. But he could not continue indefinitely, screwed around on his chair in this uncomfortable attitude. He turned back to Concetta and Mario. They were talking, their heads close together, and Charles, picking up the bottle, leaned across to refill their glasses. Immediately he had an uneasy sensation that he was performing an operation which he had done before, that this scene was a static piece of the past. And, almost equally quickly, he remembered.

It was just over a year ago. For some reason he and

40

Betty and the Jacksons had gone to a nightclub. Why, he could not recall, for it must have been almost his only visit to such a place in the last fifteen years, but they had been there, the four of them in this big jazzy place. Then, too, he had been slightly befuddled as he was now. Then, too, the music had been deafening, for they had been seated next to the band, and the heat had also been considerable. He had been talking over his shoulder, to somebody. Who? The waiter? An acquaintance? It certainly was not Jackson's wife, for when he had faced the table again there had been just the three of them seated there. Betty and Phil had had their heads close together. He had picked the bottle of champagne up out of its bucket and had leaned across to fill their glasses. Then he had noticed—for he had half stood up to do this—that they were holding hands beneath the table. And then he had known for sure what he had long suspected.

Now, as he poured the wine into Concetta's and Mario's glasses, he instinctively glanced down. Concetta's hands were in her lap. Mario was twisting a piece of cloth, perhaps a handkerchief, between his. They were not in collusion against him. But, with the association of scenes, he no longer wished to go on sitting at this table. Mario was once again speaking to Concetta. He could not hear what the young man was saying, but he caught her answer.

"*No!*" she said. And again. "*No!*"

Charles asked:

"Concetta, would you care to dance?"

A few couples were moving about the center of the piazza.

"No," she said. "Mario has just asked me the same. I do not want to dance."

Charles glanced around. In the corner opposite the

41

shooting gallery was another game of skill. This was a booth at the back of which were pyramids of bent and shiny tin cans. The purpose of the game was to knock over one of the pyramids with three soft balls. Charles swallowed what was left of his wine and said to Mario:

"I'll challenge you to that game over there." He pointed toward the booth. Mario did not seem to understand, and Charles, shouting against the music, said: "We'll have a match, a competition, to see which of us is the best. Oh, Concetta, translate for him!"

She told Mario what he had said, and immediately, seriously, Mario nodded. He swallowed his wine and the three of them walked over to the booth. Charles said:

"Concetta will be the umpire."

"The . . . ?" she asked.

"You will be the judge to see that nobody cheats."

"What does he say?" Mario asked. They were in front of the booth now. He heard her answer and understood it:

"He says I am to decide which of you two is the better."

Charles put down the money for two goes, noticing as he did so that this was his last five-hundred lire note. Mario took off his jacket, folded it carefully, and laid it on the wooden ledge that formed the front of the booth. Four or five people were watching. Concetta had moved a little to one side. Charles gestured Mario to begin, but the latter made it plain that he would prefer Charles to start. So Charles picked up one of the balls and, with the motion of a baseball pitcher, hurled it at the cans opposite his end of the booth. It was too big and soft a ball for such throwing, and it missed completely. Charles turned with a laugh to Mario, who was smiling now.

"Your turn, Mario," he said.

Mario also threw with great force, the muscle of his

arm bulging beneath the cheap striped cotton of his shirt. His ball knocked down three of his cans, and he gave Concetta a smile of triumph. Charles said:

"I see I am up against an expert."

The smile had gone from Mario's lean, brown face. What handsome bastards they are, Charles thought, and he remembered a surgeon friend who, during the war, had once remarked to him that when operating on Italian prisoners he often felt that it was a sin to cut into such fine bodies. Oh well, Charles sighed to himself, as he picked up his second ball, even if he is an Adonis there's no need for him to look so damn solemn all the time.

He threw this one much more carefully and it hit his pyramid exactly in the center. All his cans were gone now except two, one at each end. After this throw he did not glance at Concetta, but watched Mario attentively. The boy threw with great care, and again he hit his pyramid. Now he had three cans left standing, one on top of two.

A single hit must knock them all down, while Charles could not hope to get both his with the one ball that remained. Mario had turned again toward Concetta. Charles said:

"It looks like being yours, Mario."

Half a dozen people watched expectantly as Charles threw. He knocked over one of his remaining cans.

"Bene!" said the proprietor of the booth courteously.

Mario was concentrating on his throw. Charles saw the muscles of his jaw tighten, and then he threw. He missed the three cans completely. An expression of deepest chagrin, of childish rage, crossed his face. Without a word he picked up his jacket and began to walk away. Concetta called:

"Mario!"

And Charles repeated:

43

"Heigh, Mario!"

Somebody laughed. Mario did not turn around:

"Buona notte!" he called over his shoulder.

Once again, almost beseechingly, Concetta called after him:

"Mario!"

But he did not turn back, and the band had struck up again. For a moment Charles thought to run after him. The last thing he had intended to do was to offend the boy. But he shrugged his shoulders. He said to Concetta:

"What's the matter with him?"

"He hates to lose, at anything. Here the people all laugh because he hates so much to lose."

"I didn't want to hurt his feelings."

"Of course not. He is a silly boy. He is always so jealous."

"Oh." Charles looked down into her face. "Would you like to dance now?"

"Yes."

But he had only just put his arm around her waist when up above them three purple rockets arched across the night sky. At the top of their parabola they burst, each discharging a half dozen silver lights that began to float down, each of these latter bursting in its turn into six red ones that disappeared slowly behind the houses. The band had stopped playing, for the musicians, too, were gazing skyward.

"It's . . . unbelievable," said Charles in the sudden hush. He took Concetta's arm. "We must go somewhere where we can follow them all the way down."

Concetta said:

"The beach?"

A number of people were already headed for the stairs that led downward. Charles said:

"I think we would see them better from above. Do you feel like climbing all those steps?"

"Oh, yes."

And so they made their way slowly up to the road, stopping whenever a cluster of fireworks was set off. The band had begun to play again. Soon they were above the point of discharge of the rockets, but they went on up. At the top the road was deserted.

They leaned their elbows on the low wall. Beneath them the lights of the village twinkled, and they could see the people, small as minnows, dancing in the piazza to the now distant music of the band. Down on the beach, Adelmo's terrace was a patch of brightness; beyond, the sea shimmered silkily. A flight of green rockets rose, very slowly it seemed, and discharged a golden rain over it all. They said nothing, waiting for what would happen next. Green, lemon, deepest red, silver and blue the rockets went up in honor of the patron saint. Down below the band played on. Charles took Concetta in his arms and kissed her.

"Carlo!" she murmured. "Carlo!"

Chapter Four

THE BEACH FACED SOUTH, and at either end there rose high and cliffy headlands. That to the east was surmounted by a ruined tower, called by the local inhabitants the "English tower," though it had been built by the natives in the middle ages as a lookout and refuge against

the ever-threatening Corsairs. But Nelson had visited
Siano, coming by barge in the congenial company of
Sir William and Lady Hamilton, and had somehow
acquired a titular right to what was even then a ruin.
According to some, the English party had simply pic-
nicked on the greensward. Others said that the admiral
had there erected a gallows, from which he had hanged
four liberals, and left them hanging, as a warning to
any Francophile republicans in the village below who
might have forgotten their duty to their obese Bourbon
monarch. Since then it had been known as the English
tower.

There were two routes to the English tower. A rough
path led up from the beach, a difficult and sinuous
scramble through gorse and boulders; while from the
uncompleted road above the town it was possible to
reach it over almost level ground. It was on account of
these two approaches that Concetta had proposed it as
their meeting place. She would go up by way of the town.
It would not be thought odd if Charles were to be seen
climbing the cliff path on the afternoon following the
festa.

Usually Charles had had a swim before old Maria
arrived with his morning coffee and buttered bread.
Today she found him asleep, though she, too, was late.
Somewhat blearily he drank the coffee. She seemed to
be a very long time in leaving. At last, by the door, she
began to speak. He could not follow what she said, for
she talked with a very strong local accent, but he heard
the word *tass* or *tasse* repeated several times.

"*Bene, Maria, bene,*" he said. With a last, doubtful
glance at him, she left the room and he jumped out of
bed.

Twenty minutes later, shaved and wearing only his

bathing trunks, with a towel slung about his neck, he ran down to the water's edge. He swam for a long time; when he came out, only slightly short of breath, his head was quite clear. He looked up and down the beach. He had no desire to paint today. Almost for the first time since arriving at Siano, he wished that there was someone with whom he could talk in his own language. Although it could still be barely more than half past ten, he decided he would go to the café and drink a bottle of wine. He picked up his cigarettes and matches. *"Buon giorno, Mario!"* he said, as he passed the boat, where Mario and his father were working. Mario did not look up. For a moment Charles stood there; then he shrugged his shoulders and walked on. He glanced up at the English tower, outlined against the brilliant, morning sky.

The terrace was deserted, but the débris of the night before had all been swept away.

"Adelmo!" he called. And from inside came the landlord's voice:

"Subito!"

"Bring me a bottle of white wine . . . *Subitissimo* . . ."

Charles sat down at one of the tables and lit a cigarette. Adelmo, wearing once again his dark, collarless shirt and his dark unbuttoned waistcoat, appeared almost immediately with the yellow bottle of ice-cold wine and a glass. Charles said:

"If you enjoyed the *festa* as much as I did, Adelmo, I imagine you could do with a glass yourself. Won't you join me?"

"How's that?"

"Oh, come on. Get yourself a glass and sit down."

On the table lay a pack of cards. Charles pulled them toward him. Adelmo had not moved. He was looking at Charles with an expression that seemed to be one of embarrassment on his face. Charles felt a certain mounting apprehension. He said:

"Would you like a game of *scopa?*"

Now Adelmo said:

"Mister Charles, I hate bother you . . . You remember what I said yesterday, about the money. The people, they worried . . . Maria . . . the tobacconist . . . they ask me if you know yet when your money come. . . ."

Charles breathed with relief. He had feared something altogether different. And it was almost casually that he replied:

"Tell them not to worry. I explained to you yesterday, it'll come. . . ."

But this did not satisfy Adelmo. He said, with an edge of roughness to his voice:

"Mister Charles, the people here they not rich people. Me myself you owe fifty thousand lire. I know you pay me, but . . ."

Charles, shuffling the cards between his fingers, looked up into Adelmo's unshaven face. He was beginning to feel slight irritation, though he did his best to conceal it.

"Of course I'll pay. What do they think I'm going to do? Run away in the middle of the night with my suitcases on my back?"

And he laughed shortly. But Adelmo went on:

"Two years ago there was a foreigner here. Like you, he owe everybody money, me, everybody else. One morning he gets in his car and he's gone. I know you don't do that, but the others . . ."

"And I suppose you put your brilliant carabinieri on his trail and nothing was ever heard of him again. . . . Anyhow, I haven't got a car."

Charles poured himself a glass of wine. Now Adelmo sat down opposite him. He said:

48

"I sorry. But the people here . . . Maria, she gotta pay her taxes now. . . ."

"Listen. I waited ten days for your policemen to get me back my checks. Then I wrote to the Express Company. They have to clear it through their New York office. As soon as that's been done they'll send me the money. It may be tomorrow, it may be in two weeks. It's as embarrassing for me as it is for you, more so. But what else can I do?"

He took a swallow of his wine. Adelmo said:

"Maybe you got friends can lend you money till your checks arrive . . . ?"

But Charles was not listening. Concetta had appeared in the frame of the door. She was wearing her simple, white cotton dress and was outlined against the dark beading of the metallic curtain. For perhaps two whole seconds Charles looked at her and she at him, and he felt a grave wonder and astonishment rising within him. "Am I in love? Am I in love with this beautiful girl in this hot and beautiful place?" That question, and what had happened last night, were the reality, not this ridiculous, repetitive conversation about money and checks.

Adelmo's reality was something else. Since his back was to the door, he had seen only the change on Charles's face. Now he half-swiveled in his chair and his expression immediately toughened, becoming almost savage. Concetta disappeared at once through the curtain, which continued to rattle a little. Adelmo turned back to face Charles, and the latter, to cover his nervousness began to fiddle with the pack of cards.

"Have you ever seen a Tarot pack?" he said. "They're the ancestors of these ones, I suppose. Only they have extra cards, the Emperor, the Hanged Man, the Wizard. They are used for telling fortunes. . . ."

49

"Mister Charles, what you want me tell these people about the money?"

Charles sighed:

"I'll send a couple of cables, one to Naples about the checks . . . and one to my . . . to America for a little money to tide me over. Does that satisfy you?"

"Thank you. Is best you do that. When can you get reply?"

"Let's see. Today's Wednesday, isn't it? The reply should be here Friday, maybe even tomorrow, say Saturday at the latest."

Adelmo looked slightly more cheerful now. Charles swallowed his drink, and refilled his glass. He said:

"I'll go to the telegraph office right away. Only . . . I've just remembered . . . I haven't got any money at all now. Can you lend me two or three thousand lire to pay for the cables?"

Charles had got to his feet. Slowly Adelmo put his hand in his pocket and took out a thin wad of greasy notes. He peeled off two, which he handed to Charles.

"You give back soon . . . ?"

"Of course," said Charles impatiently. "As soon as the money arrives. Put this bottle back on ice for me, will you? Thanks, Adelmo."

And he walked away.

Adelmo watched him until he had disappeared around the corner. Adelmo's eyes were calculating; he was not smiling.

The steps were in shadow, so that when he emerged into the piazza, the paving stones were a shock to his bare feet and the sun beat down upon his torso. Here, too, the decorations for the *festa* had been taken away with remarkable speed; the booths were all gone; no

50

doubt the vendors had moved on to some other village that was honoring some other saint. There was nobody about save an old woman and the younger of the two carabinieri, lounging, in his brown uniform once again, outside the *municipio*. His head filled with thoughts of Concetta, Charles walked across the piazza.

"Signore!" said the policeman, stepping forward and touching the peak of his cap. Charles stopped and gazed at the man, who immediately broke into a long sentence. Charles could not understand.

"Prego?" he asked. The policeman repeated his remarks in a more authoritative tone, but again Charles failed to understand. It would have been a deadlock, had not the village priest now walked down the steps that led from the church. His old eyes were fixed on Charles with evident disapproval as he approached. When he was within a few yards the policeman addressed him respectfully, but with a certain urgency. The priest stopped at once. Charles smiled; the smile was not returned. The priest, speaking a very pure English with only the slightest Italian accent said:

"Are you an Englishman?"

Charles was somewhat taken aback. It had never occurred to him that the priest might speak English. He said:

"No, Father, I'm American." And then: "Can you tell me what this man is trying to say to me?"

The priest eyed him coolly. He replied at last:

"He wishes you to know that it is against the law to walk the streets without clothes. It is also indecent."

Charles felt a blush beginning to rise to his cheeks. He said:

"Oh, I'm sorry. I didn't know. I won't do it again." And then to the policeman: "Excuse me . . . *scusi . . .*"

51

The priest looked stonily at Charles before walking on. Had the priest said a single word, or given a single glance that showed understanding for Charles's harmless mistake, Charles would have gone down to his room on the beach and put on shirt and trousers. But he had simply walked on, his black soutane rustling. The policeman had moved back to the shady wall, against which he was leaning once again as he picked his teeth. The incident was closed, save that Charles felt humiliated. It had been an affront.

Angrily he pushed open the door of the post office, where the postmistress's large, ugly face filled the small window in the frosted glass screen that divided the room in two. There was a large mole on the side of her nose. Brusquely Charles asked for two telegraph forms. She handed them to him without a word. When he had written his telegrams, she kept him waiting for some minutes while she finished making an entry in a large ledger with a scratchy steel pen.

That afternoon it was hotter than ever, and the faint breeze from the south was no relief. From over the sands of the Sahara and the glassy waters of the Mediterranean it wafted only the leaden heat of the distant furnace where it was born.

When Charles got up from his bed, after his siesta, he was wringing wet. He sluiced himself down with cold water, though it was in truth almost tepid, and brushed his teeth before putting on a pair of white trousers and a blue shirt. He decided he must wear a hat, and thus he set off along the beach, which offered now no shade whatever against the fiery rays of the sun. At the end of the beach, however, beyond the last house, there was a shadowy corner, and Charles decided he would stop for a cooler moment before beginning the steep climb up the cliff.

It was a rank sort of place, with long grasses growing up about two large and broken blocks of old concrete. Charles sat down on one of these and mopped his forehead. He had been seated there for a minute or two, and was about to move on, when he heard a faint noise behind him. He looked around and could see nothing. Getting up, he glanced over the top of the other concrete block and there, in the coarse grass, was little Luigi. Charles's face lit up.

"Luigi!" he said, but immediately he saw that something was wrong. The child stared at him dully, and Charles noticed that for once he had not got his ball with him. Had the other children taken it away again? And why had not Luigi run up to him, as he always did, when first Charles had entered this little corner, for he must have seen him?

"Luigi!"

But still the boy said nothing. Charles leaned down lower, and at once, automatically, he was not just the man-on-holiday going to meet a girl on a clifftop. There were dark rings about the child's eyes and a pearly sweat on his face. Charles picked him up and placed him on the concrete block, so that he might have a better look at him. Without a doubt the child was running a temperature. He should certainly not be left sitting here, in this musty place. Charles felt his pulse and looked into the child's eyes. The boy let him do what he wished with him, unresisting and trustful, but there was nothing much in these circumstances that even the finest diagnostician could do. He could not even be sure that Luigi's eyes were, in fact, not focussing properly. Nor had Charles forgotten the unnecessary alarm that he had caused a couple of summers ago, at home, when he had thought to see the first symptoms of poliomyelitis in his own son. That had turned out, after the boy had been rushed to hospital, to be nothing but a touch of summer flu. Charles felt a momentary irritation at his own unscientific reaction. Two years ago, when his own son had shown just these symptoms, there had been an epidemic of poliomyelitis in New England. He had no reason to believe that there was one in Italy now.

No doubt Luigi had had too much candy at the *festa* yesterday. But the boy must be got home and put to bed. He was not sure where Luigi lived. He picked him up and carried him around the corner, into the glare of the beach. Luigi whimpered slightly, as Charles knocked on the door of the first house.

He recognized the tousled woman who opened it.

"Luigi!" she said and immediately took the child from him, amid a flood of words. The boy had begun to cry and Charles could not understand what the woman said, as she lowered Luigi to the ground, save that she kept repeating the word *cattivo*. But Charles did not think that Luigi was naughty. He must explain to this woman, whom he assumed to be the mother, that the child was sick and should go to bed.

"*Luigi malato,*" he said. "*Letto.*"

"*Si, si, signore. E molto cattivo,*" said the woman, pushing the little boy through the door.

Charles thought that she should get a doctor to look at the child. From the dark room behind her there came a slightly rancid smell of stale milk and fish. He said:

"*Dottore per Luigi.*"

Damn it, he thought, why haven't I learned the language properly in the three weeks I've been here?

"*Si, signore. Grazie, grazie.*"

54

Did she understand that she must send for the doctor, or was she merely expressing her realization of the fact that he, Charles, was a medical man? He could not tell for sure. Luigi was standing half behind her skirts, his great, dark eyes fixed on Charles. Charles did not see how he could make his meaning clear to the woman. Besides, it was probably just a case of overeating and over-excitement. He would get Adelmo to act as his interpreter when he went to the café that evening. Once again, firmly, he said:

"Letto!" and she seemed to understand. Then he turned away and walked towards the base of the cliff. Poor little fellow, he thought to himself, as he began the rough climb, poor little Luigi.

Up on the balcony above Adelmo's café the old man sat, as he did each afternoon, his binoculars on the table before him.

At half past three he watched Charles come out of his room and walk along the beach. He was surprised to see the foreigner disappear behind the last house at the end. He was still more surprised, excited even, to see him come out again, five minutes later, carrying a child. Ah, it was the Spinta child! The mother was not a good woman. She had been little better than a whore, in the old days, when the soldiers were here. The man was knocking at her door, yes, there she was, untidy as ever. He was sure her house must be filthy inside, Spinta had been a fool ever to marry the woman. And now she was talking to this other foreigner, bah! But look, she hasn't asked the foreigner into her house. He is gesticulating— too dirty even for him, eh? And those lecherous brutes will put up with anything. And now he is going away, *that* way. Where can he be going?

55

The old man breathed on the glass of his binoculars, rubbed the lenses against his trousers, and raised them to his eyes once again.

Climbing the cliff! To the English tower! A stiff climb. Yes, the old man had thought he wouldn't be able to keep up that pace for long. Now he has sat down on a boulder. What is he doing? Ah, he is taking something from his pocket. A packet of cigarettes. He lights one. The old man scratched under his armpit and when he raised the binoculars again the foreigner was still sitting on the rock. Why doesn't he hurry up and go wherever it is he is going? Perhaps he may fall and break his leg, his neck? It is fifty years since the old man has climbed that path. It used to be dangerous. Now he is going up again, the small figure in the round circle that is blurred about the edges.

He has nearly reached the top. Yes, he is over the edge. He stops and looks about him. What can he be searching for? There is nothing up there, not even sheep any more. But he must have seen whatever he wants to see, for he is walking off rapidly toward the English tower. And now he is out of sight. What a pity! But the old man has plenty of time, the whole afternoon in fact, the whole of the rest of his life. Every few minutes the old man raised his binoculars.

At five o'clock the old man awoke from a brief doze. He glanced along the beach. The fishermen were getting ready their boats. They would be going out tonight, though the old man felt, indeed knew, that a sirocco was blowing up. Well, tonight should be all right. Then, suddenly, he remembered the foreigner at the top of the cliff. Perhaps he had gone up there to commit suicide, like that other foreigner so many years ago? Adelmo had told him he owed money to everybody in the village, tens of thousands of lire, a madman, a lunatic. Perhaps he had already jumped off the cliff, three hundred feet straight down onto the rocks and water? But no, even now there was something moving up there, something white.

The old man raised his binoculars. It is, it can't be! yes, it is his granddaughter, Concetta. For perhaps twenty seconds she is within his vision, coming from behind the tower in the circle of the glass, before the slope hides her. And now, yes, yes, now there is the foreigner. He, too, is coming from the tower, making for the cliff path.

The binoculars trembled in the old man's hands.

"Adelmo!" he called, as loudly as he could. "Adelmo!"

PART II

Chapter One

MONEY STOLEN PLEASE CABLE ME FIVE HUNDRED DOLLARS IMMEDIATELY LOVE CHARLES.

It was five o'clock in the evening on Long Island. Betty Warren left the children on the tennis court, while she and Phil Jackson went into the big, chintz-fitted drawing-room of her mother's house. She threw her racket on the sofa and sat down, with a sigh, in one of the four or five deep armchairs. Phil sniffed at a bowl of roses. They were hot-house grown; he knew this, for he had bought them himself, in New York, that morning.

"Ho!" said Betty. "I'm thirsty. Let's have some tea."

From outside came the thin voices of the children. Here, too, summer had arrived.

Phil Jackson walked across and stroked her hair. But she was not in the mood for affection. Her admirable legs in the white shorts were stuck out straight in front of her.

"Ring the bell, over there by the door, will you?"

After he had done so he sat down in another armchair. She said:

"The most extraordinary cable just arrived from Charles."

"Yes? How's he getting on?"

"It's hard to say. He hasn't written me." She sat up, reached for the cable that was behind the silver cigarette box, and handed it across to him. "Tell me what you make of this."

He took it from her, and read:

HONEY SOLEP PLEASE JAPIE ME FIUE NUMBRE DOLLARS ILLEN ATELY LOUE CHARLES.

The colored maid entered the room.

"Oh, Louise, would you get us some tea, please? Well, Phil, what do you make of it?"

"I didn't know 'honey' was among his terms of endearment. Perhaps he wants some dollars. At least the Italians know how to spell that one. And the word before looks like number. I don't know, it's pure gibberish. What is 'iapie.' Happy? Perhaps he's ill? Ill in Italy? I don't know."

"I don't see why he'd want any money, he took five thousand dollars with him. He can hardly have spent that in a month."

"Maybe he wants to come home. Maybe he's homesick. I'm just guessing. What are you going to do about it?"

"I suppose I'd better cable him to find out. There's a pencil and some paper on the desk over there. Would you pass them to me, darling?"

She wrote:

CHARLES WARREN SIANO NEAR NAPLES ITALY YOUR CABLE QUITE INCOMPREHENSIBLE BETTY.

"I don't see why I should put in 'love,' do you?"

"Why not compromise with 'loue'?"

They both laughed.

"Oh, Louise, put the tea down on the table here, will you? Thank you. Do you want lemon in yours, Phil?"

60

A bee hummed loudly. From outside came the voices of the children.

At that moment it was a little after ten o'clock at Siano. Charles sat in his room, reading by the light of the oil lamp. He had brought few books with him. He read:

The bay trees in our country are all wither'd
And meteors fright the fixed stars of heaven,
The pale-fac'd moon looks bloody on the earth
And lean-looked prophets whisper fearful change,
Rich men look sad and ruffians dance and leap,
The one in fear to lose what they enjoy . . .

He closed the volume over his forefinger and gazed about the bare room. It was many years since he had last read Shakespeare, not since Princeton, in fact, and the familiar, forgotten words, combined with the events of the evening, made his passion of the afternoon and of the night before seem almost improbable. He lit a cigarette, placed the book on the bare, deal table beside his shaving things, and thought.

If I stay here, I shall without any doubt whatever fall in love with Concetta. Indeed, I have almost if not quite done so already. That will mean one of two things: either I must break up my marriage, or I shall have to . . . to what? He rubbed his knuckles across his forehead. He tried to visualize Concetta in New York, in his apartment. It was not difficult. But the children . . . Well, other people got divorces, remarried and the rest of it. Oh, exactly, and that had precisely nothing whatever to do with it. Have you heard about Dr. Warren? Went off to Italy, became infatuated with some peasant girl, and now by God he's married her and brought her back to New York! So what? So what would Concetta do all day long?

61

Would his friends be her friends? Well, he'd damn well get some new friends. Where? Perhaps he could put an advertisement in *The Times*. "Middle-aged doctor recently married eighteen-year-old Italian peasant girl desires set new friends guaranteed not to make child bride feel unwanted and strange." His mother would be sweet to Concetta, almost incredibly sweet, so that even she would not believe it. And the children . . .

Yes, it could be done. Or he could go away, now, at once, as soon as his money arrived. Then he must tell Concetta, now, at once. But why? When it was so sweet, so perfect. *Carpe diem* and so on. Did he not owe himself a little pleasure? No, he didn't. That wasn't at all the point. Besides . . .

Besides, was it sweet and perfect? He glanced out of the window. The fishing fleet had put to sea, and now the boats were strung across the horizon, each with its light moving gently in the darkness. The south wind soughed gently along the beach. Was it?

Adelmo had brought him his evening meal at the café. Was it just the money that made him so stiff, almost surly? They had gone together to the Spinta woman's house, but Adelmo had replied only in monosyllables to Charles's attempts at conversation. He had translated, had stood by while Charles took the boy's temperature with Adelmo's thermometer, had telephoned the doctor from the café. The doctor, he had informed Charles, lived some twelve miles away, but would attempt to come to Siano in the course of the following day. Then, abruptly, Adelmo had turned on his heel and walked out of the café, into the private part of the house. Since the inn was deserted, all the men being out with the fishing fleet, there was nobody for him to serve save Charles. This he apparently had no wish to do; Charles had therefore come back to his room and was reading *Richard II*. The obvious conclusion was that he knew or suspected something about Concetta. So? Hardly the atmosphere in which to pluck days, to have a brief and idyllic love affair. Even if that were what he wished to have. Even if he were prepared to ignore all possible consequences to the girl. Even if . . .

There was a tap on the window pane. He got up and opened the door. It was Concetta.

"Carlo, please come out. I must talk to you. Please come at once. I daren't come in."

He closed the door behind him. The wind was louder out here.

"Quickly," she said. "This way."

She had taken his hand and was leading him down, across the beach, to the corner by the water's edge, at the far end from the English tower. He felt the slight roughness of her hand. When they were surely out of the faint band of light that the windows of the houses cast, she stopped and turned toward him, though without releasing his hand. She said:

"Carlo, I'm frightened. My father . . . he knows we were up on the cliff this afternoon. He is . . . so angry."

He could just see her face in the darkness, and he drew her to him. She buried her head against his chest. Above her black hair were the lights of Siano, a pyramid against the enfolding blackness of the mountains. The outline of the church dome was faintly discernible. Charles stroked her hair. He said, and his words surprised him:

"Poor Concetta!"

She drew a little away from him and looked up. She said:

"My father says you will run away and leave me. He

say Mario will not want me now, and I shall have to marry some horrible old man, like the Spinta woman, because she . . ."

Once again she buried her head against his chest, and once again he stroked her hair. He must speak now, at once, but what should he say? She was sobbing softly. She said:

"Oh, Carlo, I don't want to marry Mario . . . I don't want to be like the Spinta . . . I don't want to spend all my life here, till I'm old and ugly like those widows at the *festa*. Tell me, Carlo, tell me now, is it true you'll run away and leave me? Is it true?"

It was unbearably painful.

"I love you, Concetta." And that was true, absolutely true. "I love you, and I would marry you, Concetta, if . . ."

"Will you marry me, Carlo . . . ? Oh, Carlo, will you marry me and take me away from here?"

She had moved away from him slightly, but he held her arms above the elbows. Now that his eyes were growing more accustomed to the darkness, he could see the eagerness of her face. She had stopped crying. The wind blew between them. He said, slowly and softly:

"I love you, Concetta. But you wouldn't be happy with me, not for long. . . . You wouldn't understand the sort of life I lead in New York. Do you see, Concetta? You would be unhappy and then you would stop loving me and you would wish I had never taken you away from Siano."

"No!" she said emphatically. "It's not true. I will be happy with you. I won't be in your way. I promise. I'll cook for you and look after you and I'll never do anything you don't like. I know I'm only an ignorant girl, but I'll study and learn and you won't have to be ashamed of me, I promise. I promise you, Carlo!"

64

Charles let go her arms. For a moment he was silent, and then he said, very slowly:

"Concetta . . . I am married already. I should have told you before."

He felt the wind blowing little flurries of sand about his ankles. One of the lights in the town went out. There was the sound of water slapping against the rocks at the base of the cliff. When she spoke, her voice was low and level. She said:

"Yes, you should have told me. Not to have told me is like lying."

And now that he had lost her, he knew that he was truly in love with her. He said:

"Yes, it was like lying. But, Concetta, it's not a real marriage any more. It . . . How could I have told you about my wife? How can I tell you now? It's a different world from this one. I may be married to her, but it is you I love. That is why . . ."

He stopped. She said, levelly:

"Like those soldiers loved the Spinta woman."

"Please, Concetta, you must understand . . ."

"I understand. Now kiss me, Carlo. Kiss me once more. Please."

He took her in his arms and kissed her. All his limbs felt weak and there was a sick hollowness within him. He lifted her head and looked down at her, the great dark eyes in the blur of white that was her face. He bent his head to kiss her once again, but she turned away and slipped out of his arms. She said:

"No!"

"Concetta, darling, kiss me once again."

"No. It's finished. I'm going back now."

"But . . ."

She took two steps backward, away from him. For a

65

second she was there before him, then quickly she was walking away. He began, automatically, to follow her, but soon stopped. For a long time her white dress was visible, growing smaller. Then she crossed the patch of light that was the café terrace and vanished. Nothing was left save the deserted beach, and the slapping of the water against the rocks, and the fishing fleet far out to sea, and the lights of the town that were going out one by one, and the soughing of the wind. Charles felt the hollowness growing within him. He shuddered.

Chapter Two

ALL NEXT DAY the south wind blew, rasping over the sand, exacerbating human nerves and apparently those of animals as well, for a dog, tied up somewhere out of sight, howled ceaselessly. It was not a very strong wind, but steady and hot. Waves rolled in toward the shore; they in their turn churned up the sandy bottom, so that the sea became the color of stale, tepid tea to which milk has been added half an hour before. There were flecks of white on the broken waves which, only as they neared the shore, joined together to build a petty line of breakers. In its travels across the Sahara this wind had drawn up a mass of fine dust which crept through the cracks of door and window and imperceptibly irritated lungs and eyeballs. There were no clouds, but the dust in the sky enlarged and reddened the sun which now glared heavily down upon the houses and the beach.

The fishermen's catch had been a poor one the night before. Along that coast there are few true sailors, and now they pulled their boats high up the sand, cursing and stumbling at their clumsy task. The wind blew.

For the first time since being in Siano Charles had been unable to sleep. At last, and reluctantly, he had taken one of his sleeping pills. When Maria woke him with his coffee, the brown and bitter taste of the barbiturate still lingered in his mouth. His few hours of sleep had been only a period of unconsciousness; if he had dreamed, the dream was gone at once. He awoke immediately to the reality of the night before, a reality of failure and of self-disgust that exactly matched the taste on his tongue. He got up and brushed his teeth, but his head still ached slightly as he forced himself to drink the coffee that was not hot enough and eat the buttered rounds of bread.

The decision was made, and not by him. Today, presumably, his money would arrive. He would pay his bills and leave right away. But where to? The decision that he had made was to come here. Now he must make another and he had not the heart to do so. He rubbed his hands over his face; his skin felt old, his flesh flabby. The wind rattled the window panes, through which he could see the fishermen struggling about their boats or walking up the beach bent beneath the weight of their gear. With a sigh he got to his feet and began to busy himself with his packing. It would at least stop him from thinking about Concetta.

He would put on his gray flannel suit, so that he need not change again. When he took it from the cupboard he saw that there was a stain down the front, and he remembered then the glass of wine that he had spilled on the night of the *festa*. It seemed an age ago, as he tried, with face cloth and water, to remove it. All he succeeded in doing was to make the patch larger and darker. Oh, well. He laid the jacket on one side and went on with his packing. There was not much to pack, it was soon done. After these weeks of wearing rope soles his brown leather shoes felt very stiff and heavy. Once his things had been put away in the two suitcases stacked by the door with his overcoat folded on top of them, this room, which had been for a short time his home, had become utterly impersonal again. It too, he thought, rejected him, in the callous and sordid manner of hotel rooms with their unmade beds and toothpaste-spotted washbasins.

He sat down again at the table and lit a cigarette, noticing as he did so that he had only seven left. Should he go for a walk on this glaring, windy day? Then he remembered little Luigi and that memory was a sort of life-belt to him. He was a good and conscientious doctor, not a dishonest seducer with bad nerves washed up on an alien shore. His office was there, within reach almost, clean and orderly, and he was Doctor Warren, competent and helpful and respected. He got to his feet, put on the jacket with the great, dark stain running down one side, and went out into the persistent wind. The heels of his shoes sank into the sand, so that walking itself was strange.

It was Luigi's mother who opened the door to him. Her face was grimy and streaked with tears, her hair more untidy than the day before, but she did attempt to give him a smile as she invited him in. It was a room not unlike his own farther along the beach, though dirty and crowded. In the center stood a great square table, covered with a red cloth on which were remnants of a meal, and clothing and even a pair of boots. Scattered around this table were chairs, one with a broken leg lying on its side,

68

and packing cases. In the corner stood a clothes-maker's dummy with a wasp waist. At the back, half hidden by a red curtain, he could see the end of a great wooden double bed, and nearer the door was a smaller bed or cot on which lay the little boy, Luigi. But for the moment Charles could not see Luigi, for there were two men between him and the cot.

They turned toward him as he came in, a fisherman in late middle age with yellow stumpy teeth, whom Charles remembered seeing at the *festa,* and another, much older man, who could only be the doctor. For this latter was dressed in a black frock coat, such as Charles had only seen in pictures or in the movies. His head was a white, hairless skull, and around his neck there was slung an old-fashioned stethoscope. He held a large thermometer in his hand and beside him, on the table among the scraps of food, was a black doctor's bag of cracked patent leather, the trademark of the profession two or three generations ago. Luigi's mother spoke quickly to this venerable figure, who then bowed toward Charles and said something which the latter could not understand.

Now it is always embarrassing for a doctor to interfere or even to appear to interfere, in a case that a colleague is handling. Charles's immediate reaction was to return the bow and withdraw. Yet there was something so incompetent-looking about this relic of the nineteenth century that he felt he would be negligent if he did not at least offer a few suggestions. He said to the doctor, while the parents stared from the one to the other:

"Do you speak English?"

"*Non, monsieur,*" came the creaking, rusty reply, "*mais je parle français.*"

This was a little better, and for the rest of their conversation they spoke in French, though Charles's knowl-

69

edge of the language was inadequate. He apologized for interrupting the old man's diagnosis, explained that he was himself a diagnostician and told the doctor that it was he who had found the boy yesterday afternoon and that he feared he might be seriously ill. The faces of the parents were strained as they tried to follow the foreign words. The aged doctor was about to reply, when the boy on the cot gave a low moan, and they all automatically looked toward him.

The child's face was flushed, his silken hair dark and matted with sweat, and he kept moving his head slowly from side to side. Charles leaned down. The boy's eyes were glazed and vacant and he did not show any sign that he recognized his friend. Then Charles straightened up. He knew that he must be tactful with the old man, that he must put the suggestions into his mouth. He therefore asked him what he thought the malady to be.

"Influenza," said the doctor, addressing Charles as *cher confrère*. "The child had influenza. Do you not agree, *cher confrère?*"

Charles said that at first glance it did not look like influenza to him.

"In that case, *cher confrère*, perhaps it is food poisoning from which the little one is suffering. In either event there is nothing that we can do, save to let the malady run its course."

Charles continued to look doubtful, and the old man went on:

"But I will do what I can. Tomorrow I shall come again and give the little one an injection of penicillin."

"Doctor," said Charles, "I think it is not impossible that that child may have meningitis or poliomyelitis. I think he should be taken to hospital for observation at once."

Now the doctor laughed, a mirthless sound.

"Poliomyelitis! It is all the rage in America, is it not, your poliomyelitis? Twenty years ago it was appendicitis, now all we read about in your magazines is polio, polio, polio. No, no, *cher confrère*, we are not now in New York City. The child has influenza, or perhaps he has eaten something that disagrees with his poor little insides."

The boy moaned again, softly. His mother leaned down and stroked his brow, but did not take her eyes from the doctors' faces. Charles said:

"Doctor, would you come outside for a moment?"

The old man raised his non-existent eyebrows, but followed him into the hot, persistent wind. At considerable length Charles explained, as best he could in his defective French, why he thought that the child might have meningitis or even polio, and why if there was even the slightest risk of it, he should be taken to hospital at once for isolation and a laboratory investigation of the cerebro-spinal fluid. When at last he had finished, the old man said:

"I see you think you know my business better than I do. Perhaps in America with your machines and your drugs you would be a better doctor than I am." Charles tried to interrupt him, to say that that was far from what he meant, but the old doctor plowed steadily on, like a rusty old tram running along rusty lines. "But here, *cher confrère*, I am the doctor. I have looked after these people, yes, and their fathers and their grandfathers, for nearly sixty years. I understand their maladies. They do not suffer from these fashionable complaints. Tomorrow I shall give the child this new drug, penicillin, though it is a pure waste of money. It may help his influenza, at least it will not do him any harm. But as to moving the

71

child to the hospital at Naples, it is ridiculous. Besides, the parents could not afford it."

"If that's what is stopping you, I'll pay."

Once again an expression of some astonishment crossed the skull-like features.

"You will pay, sir? And why should you pay?"

"Because," said Charles, "it seems to me scandalous to leave the child here when there is at least a danger that he has a virulent and highly infectious disease."

The doctor laughed softly, and Charles realized now that he had done exactly what he did not intend to do, that he had offended the old man.

"Very well, sir," said the doctor, "if you are prepared to pay the bill, and if the parents are agreeable, I shall see whether it is possible to secure a bed in the hospital. For here in Italy we cannot bundle sick children about the countryside at the mere whim of visiting foreigners, you know. Perhaps in America that is possible, but here the parents have a little say in how their children will be looked after. And by whom."

"I am extremely sorry. The last thing I want to do is to interfere—"

"Really?" the doctor asked.

"Yes, really. But I do feel, indeed I am sure, that it would be both wiser and safer if the child could be moved to hospital immediately."

"I fear that even your money cannot arrange that. First I must make the necessary arrangements with the hospital authorities—who are understaffed and who do not care to admit patients suffering only from minor indispositions. Then, if they can accept the case, they will arrange for an ambulance to be sent." And he smiled.

The old bastard, Charles thought, but he managed to say nothing. The doctor said:

"Meanwhile, are you prepared to cover the costs of the child's treatment, the hospital fees, the penicillin and so on?"

"Yes, certainly."

"In that case, perhaps you would not mind giving me a deposit of fifty thousand lire?"

"Surely that is most irregular?"

"Irregular, sir? Are you accusing me of irregularity? Am I to expose the hospital to the risk of losing money merely on the word of a foreigner? How am I to know that you are a doctor at all?"

The argument seemed to Charles to have become as preposterous as it was unpleasant. He said, curtly:

"When you have arranged for the child's admission to the hospital, I shall give the deposit that you require to the hospital authorities."

"And my own bill? Not all doctors are millionaires, you know."

"You'll be paid," said Charles, wondering already what was the Italian medical body to which he could report this repulsive old man.

"Very well," said the doctor, and the two of them re-entered the cramped, untidy room. An obese cat jumped off the table from among the scraps of food.

The aged doctor made what seemed to Charles a long speech to the parents, occasionally pointing at the sick child and once or twice at Charles. When he came to the word *ospedale,* which he repeated twice and ominously, the mother collapsed into a chair.

"No!" she said, burying her face in her hands. *"No!"*

The old doctor shrugged his shoulders and turned toward Charles, an expression of satisfaction on his face. But now the fisherman began to speak, slowly and hesitantly. It was clear to Charles that he was agreeing,

73

that he did not object to the boy being taken to the hospital.

The doctor began again. The mother was gazing up into his face. At one point she turned her eyes to Charles and said:

"Grazie!"

Then Charles knew that it was decided. He felt it was time he left. He bowed to the old doctor, apologized once again for his interference and walked out. By his firmness, he knew, he had done everything that lay within his power for the child, and perhaps also for the village of Siano. This knowledge, as he walked back along the beach, his feet sinking into the sand with every step he took, was at least something to set against the humiliation of last night. And therefore he found he had the courage, which he felt he might otherwise have lacked, to go to Adelmo's for his midday meal. Somewhere out of sight the dog was still howling at the hot wind.

The terrace of the café was deserted. The wind would have blown the checked cloths right off the tables, had they not been fastened to the edges by metal clips. As it was, they slapped and fluttered steadily. From inside there came the hum of voices. Charles pushed his way through the metal curtain. As usual it took a moment or so before his eyes became accustomed to the comparative darkness. During this moment the men seated at the tables, the fishermen deprived of their livelihood by the cursed sirocco, fell silent.

He caught just a glimpse of Concetta's back, as she disappeared through the door at the far end of the room; and then he saw Adelmo walking toward him, between the tables, all of which were occupied by the silent men.

"What you want?" asked Adelmo roughly.

"I came for my lunch," replied Charles steadily.

"Outside!" said Adelmo.

It was ambiguous. Charles, making an effort to keep his voice completely level, said:

"Yes, I'd like to have it on the terrace."

For a moment he thought that Adelmo was going to hit him, but he did not move. Then Adelmo turned on his heel and walked away. Charles glanced at the silent fishermen seated around the tables, some with glasses in their hands, others holding pieces of crusty bread. No eye met his. He walked out through the rattling curtain. Inside the voices began again.

He was standing with his hands on the balustrade that ran along the two sides of the terrace, when he heard the curtain moving behind him. He turned, half expecting to see Concetta, but it was Adelmo again. He was carrying in one hand a plate with bread, ham, an orange, and in the other a bottle and glass. The bottle was one that Charles had not finished the night before. He placed them on a table and then walked across to Charles.

Slowly, insultingly almost, he looked Charles up and down, from head to foot. Charles's headache had never quite gone, and he felt too hot in his gray suit. Adelmo said:

"You going away? You got your money?"

"I think it'll come this afternoon. Then I'll be going at once."

"And don't come back."

Adelmo was a good head and a half shorter than Charles. While waiting out here on the terrace, Charles had decided that he must tell Adelmo about Luigi, but this was obviously not the occasion. He said:

"Please have my bill ready."

"It's ready," said Adelmo, staring straight into the

taller man's eyes. "And don't you come back to Siano no more. We don't like you here. You understand?"

For a moment longer Adelmo stared at him. Then he walked slowly away. Charles felt nausea rising within him, yet he forced himself to sit down at the table and to eat the food that grew grittier with each mouthful. The steady wind and the glare of the sun made his headache worse, but he sat there until he had finished the wine in the bottle. Occasionally a fisherman would come out of the café and walk past him. None glanced his way. At last he went back to his room and threw himself down upon the unmade bed.

But suppose, he thought to himself, suppose the money doesn't come today? I can't ever set foot inside that café again, that's certain. I can't, for instance, say good-bye to Concetta. When I've gone away I can write to her and tell her all she meant to me, and try to explain that I'm not the sort of man she thinks I am. And when I get back to America, if my marriage really is broken, there's nothing to stop me coming to Siano and taking her away and marrying her. "We don't like you here. You understand?" Cheap little ex-gangster with his bootlegger's threats. I'm certainly not going to let that sort of thing worry me. But suppose my money doesn't come today? Well, I'll just have to hole up in this room, and walk along the beach, and visit the English tower and wait till it does come. If it's not today it'll be tomorrow. And when I've gone away, to Rome, I might as well go to Rome and stay at the Excelsior and have a hot bath and get my suit cleaned, when I've gone away I'll write to Concetta, and I'll say . . .

He sat up suddenly.

Surely she'll have the sense to cable me the money right away? Yes, of course she will. She may be several kinds of a bitch, but at least she's not vindictive or mean and God knows she's certainly not stupid.

He lay down again, after turning over the pillow which was already damp with sweat.

And when the money arrives, first of all I'll pay the bills. Then I'll phone for a taxi. Then I'll explain to that nasty little crook about Luigi. In Naples I'll go to the hospital, I think there's a Swiss hospital in Naples, and arrange for Luigi to be moved there at once. He certainly mustn't be left at the mercy of these people and that grotesque old man. Then I'll go to Rome and I'll write to Concetta and I'll say . . . And we'll go to the mountains, Concetta and I, up into the snow-covered mountains, away from this damned wind, up among the gentians and the cow bells and the houses that smell of pine, or maybe it'll be the winter and the snow will be crisp on top, and there'll be one of those tiled stoves in our bedroom, and I'll teach her how to ski, or not if she doesn't want to. Anyhow I'll ski myself, curving down the mountain side, gliding and turning and flying over the tight snow. . . .

"Signore, signore!"

It took him a long time to awake, forcing his way up through an ocean of monstrous and menacing shapes.

"Signore, signore!"

He sat up and shook his head. It was Luigi's mother who had been tugging at his shoulder, but it took him a moment to realize where he was.

She was speaking to him very fast. He could not understand any part of what she said. Her panic, however, was plain to see. She was still tugging at his arm. He got up, pushed his hair back and followed her out of the room. She was almost running as she led him to her little house along the beach. He noticed that it was nearly dark and that the sea was roaring. He must have slept for several hours.

There were two old women in the child's sickroom, as well as the boy's father. But before he even entered it, and through the soughing of the wind, he could hear the child's scream. It was a long drawn out scream, high and bestial, and only when his lungs were exhausted did he stop to draw breath. Then it began again, as he moved his head from side to side, this disgusting, terrifying sound. The little boy's eyes were wide open and his chest heaved as he drew breath to scream once more. The father sat on a chair, holding his son's hand, and the two old women in black stood behind him, their fear evident in their faces. There was no need for Charles to examine the child closely. He would die, there could be little question of that. The only thing that mattered was how best to secure a sedative, as much for the sake of the parents as of the child.

"*Telephonato? Dottore?*" he asked the father. Goddamn it, why couldn't he speak this language?

The fisherman, dazed with anguish, answered slowly. So far as Charles could understand, he had telephoned the doctor, and the answer had been *domani,* tomorrow. The son of a bitch. In that case there were only two things to do: to give the child a sleeping pill, perhaps two, which should at least dull the pain, and to telephone that hospital at Naples. Which of course, he thought, is what I should have done yesterday or at least this morning.

"*Momento!*" he said, and ran back to his own room, his feet sinking deep with every step he took, so that his shoes became filled with sand and enormously heavy.

He quickly found the pills, and ran back with the box. Sleeping pills as an anaesthetic were far from ideal, but

78

at least they would be better than nothing. He decided to give the child two.

They had a hard time forcing his teeth apart and only by massaging his throat could Charles get the little boy to swallow them. But they seemed to work. After a minute or two his screams subsided, though he continued to groan. In a little while, Charles hoped, the child might drop off to sleep. Whether or not he would ever awake again was another matter. Meanwhile he must telephone the hospital at once. He placed the box of pills upon the table.

"*Io,*" he said, "*telephonare. Dottore e ospedale.*"

The four people looked at him silently, until suddenly the mother burst into loud and noisy sobs. The father getting up to comfort her put his arms around her. The two old women watched, and Charles hurried from the room. It was quite dark now. The child's screams re-echoed in his ears as he made his way along the beach.

Adelmo come out quickly from behind his bar, as Charles entered the café. There were half a dozen men sitting about the tables, but Charles did not look at them.

"Adelmo. I've got to telephone. The little boy, Luigi . . ."

Adelmo was standing immediately in front of him, his lips twisted, holding something in his hand.

"Your telegram come, you goddamn liar."

Automatically Charles glanced down and saw the square piece of folded, yellow paper. As he took it and shoved it in his pocket, he noticed that it had been torn open.

"Adelmo, you've got to help me get through to the hospital at once."

He could see the telephone, in the hall beyond the door that led out of the bar, an old-fashioned, two-piece telephone screwed to a board against the wall, at face level.

"You don't wanna read your telegram?"

Adelmo's lips were twisted into the shape of a smile.

"Listen, Adelmo, there's a child in agony down the beach. We've got to get through to the hospital at once."

"Of course you don't wanna read your telegram. Because you know it's a fake. You ain't got no friends to send you no money. You goddamn crook. You get outa here before I bust your face in."

Slowly, without taking his eyes from Adelmo's face, Charles withdrew the telegram from his pocket and unfolded it. Then he looked down and read:

YOUR TELEGRAM QUITE INCOMPREHENSIBLE BENNY.

Adelmo was saying:

"Your friend Benny don't understand, eh? Well me, I understand all right. Get outa here."

"Listen, Adelmo, I know you don't like me, and I don't blame you. I don't know what this telegram means, but I'll find out. Meanwhile, there's a child dying in great pain. We've got to ring the hospital. If you won't help me, I'll do it on my own."

"Get outa here, you goddamn liar."

Charles raised his left hand to push past Adelmo. At the same moment the Italian struck him. Charles was a powerful man and his right caught Adelmo on the point of the chin. He seemed to be a very long time going down, while Charles wondered if he carried a gun. A knife probably, he decided, and at that moment a chair came down on his head. He spun around; there were five of them. Mario was the only one he recognized as they jumped at him. For a moment he fought back, but soon they had him on the ground. Two or three of them were holding him, while Mario and another kicked him in the face and stomach. He felt one or more teeth break and his mouth was full of blood. Adelmo was there now, and when he leaned down and struck Charles on the nose, it was the stone against the back of his head that he felt. He could not struggle and it did not occur to him to shout. Quite objectively, for the pain did not seem to belong to himself, he wondered if they were going to kill him. They were all yelling, their faces distorted and queer, and now Charles did feel an agonizing stab of pain in his side. Suddenly he was very frightened, more frightened than he had ever believed it possible for a man to be. For now he knew that they were going to kill him, that this was the end of his life. Wrenching one arm free he half raised his torso. Immediately he was struck in the face again, and his head crashed against the concrete. He felt himself losing consciousness. But not quite. He could not open his eyes, nor could he have moved a muscle, yet he knew that the blows had stopped, and the yelling too.

Then he was being picked up and carried. He felt himself thrown through the air, and his face hit the hard sand. One of them kicked him again in the side and something wet landed on the back of his neck. There was silence.

He did not know how long he lay there in this half-conscious state. It might have been minutes or hours. At last he tried to get up. He could not manage it. Slowly he crawled down to the water's edge. A sandy wave broke over him, and another. The water poured over his face and down his nose. Coughing and spluttering he managed to get to his feet. Like a drunken man he reeled across the beach toward his room. The lights of the pretty fishing village above him spun before his eyes. Twice he fell, and each time it took him several minutes to get up again. With a tremendous effort he could just make it. As he reached his bed he fainted.

Chapter Three

CHARLES, from his window, saw them coming along the beach. There were six of them: in front, Adelmo and the two carabinieri, behind, Luigi's mother and father and one of the old women who had been at the child's sickbed the night before. The wind fluttered at the women's black clothes, as they came slowly nearer. Charles knew that they were coming for him, and his swollen lips parted, but no cry escaped them. He had an urgent, animal longing to run away, to hide. There was no running away, and no place to hide. He began to raise his right hand; the stab of pain in his shoulder was immediate. For six hours, maybe longer, Charles had known that the child was dead. He could no longer tell the time; his wristwatch had been smashed the night before, but to judge by the sunshine it was early morning now. The people were coming closer, not speaking and grim.

It had been pitch dark when he had come to. He had washed some of the blood from his face with trembling hands. No bones seemed to be broken, but he thought, to judge by the pain in his side, that perhaps a rib was cracked. He had limped along the housefronts, for he had remembered at once about the child. But when he got there the child was already dead. The priest was kneeling by the bedside, and the parents, too. There were candles at his feet and head, and the priest was praying aloud. For a moment Charles had stood, swaying in the frame of the door. The priest had not looked up nor interrupted his incantations, but the mother and father of the dead boy had both seen him, and he had seen, on their faces, the hatred and the dread. The box that had contained the sleeping pills was empty on the table. He had stumbled back to his room, and there he had waited for the pain-filled night to end. The church bell had tolled a death, each heavy note buffeted by the unending wind. Charles had sat at his table, his head buried in his arms, and the invisible dog had howled steadily throughout the night, perhaps waiting, like him, for the dawn. That had been hours ago, and now they were coming. Charles got to his feet to await them. He had never felt such fear before.

They did not knock. One of the carabinieri, the *maresciallo,* was the first to enter, followed by Adelmo and the others. They almost filled the room, and Charles had to back away in order to make room. When they were all inside—no one thought to close the door—the *maresciallo* began to speak. Charles could not understand what he said. Then the *maresciallo* turned to the mother of the dead child and asked her something. She nodded and said:

"*Sì!*"

The policeman, now holding the empty box of sleeping pills in his hand, was speaking to Charles again, in a low, level, unimpassioned voice. Charles looked to Adelmo. The latter, his face closed and his voice, too, impassive, translated:

"He wants to know: did you give Luigi Spinta these drugs?"

"I gave him two sleeping pills."

Adelmo translated this into Italian. The policeman spoke, and Adelmo said:

"Only a doctor is allowed to give drugs. A proper doctor. When the real doctor arrives he'll look at the kid. If your drugs killed him, you'll be tried. Do you understand?"

"But . . ."

"Till then you're to stay here. Not to leave this room. Do you understand?"

And then the mother began to scream at him, standing absolutely still while the tears trickled down her cheeks. He knew that she was cursing him, invoking the Virgin and the saints. For perhaps a minute she went on, while the others stood in silence, their eyes fixed on Charles's face. As abruptly as she had started, she stopped. Her husband laid his hand on her shoulder. The others followed them out. One of the carabinieri said something to Charles, which Adelmo did not translate. Then he was alone again. He closed the door behind them and sat down at his table. He was trembling all over. And he repeated to himself, time after time: "How many pills were left in the box? How many pills were there left?"

At last he could get up and shave. But when he had done that, when he had painfully drawn the razor over his cut and swollen face, there was nothing for him to do save sit down at the table once again. It was only the arrival of the postman that roused him from his leaden torpor.

The postman was not smiling as he gave him the single letter, and he turned away at once, as from something disgusting. But Charles had seen the name of the Transatlantic Express Company on the envelope, and suddenly had realized consciously what he already knew: he was not utterly lost and cast out: only a few miles away there were human beings who spoke his language, to whom he could explain what had happened, who would understand, perhaps even sympathize: there, beyond the mountains, was justice and order, and it was from that world, which a minute before seemed so remote that it might have sunk into the sea, that this letter had come. It took him a little time to open it. He read:

Dear Sir:

Our New York office advises us that no checks were drawn in favor of Charles Warner during March of this year. We suggest that perhaps the American Express or some other company provided you with these checks. Yours truly, and an illegible signature.

The fools, he thought, the utter incredible stupidity of it! And his rage at these incompetent clerks who could not even transcribe a name correctly acted as a tonic to him. It sent the adrenalin coursing through his blood once again. To hell with them, he thought, to hell with them all. What right had the police to order that he, an innocent man who had only tried to help, remain in this room? He would go at once to the post office and send half a dozen cables. He would damn well get the American consul out to show these people that an American citizen can't be treated in this way.

But the stimulus was not of long duration. By the time he had looked in the mirror, seen his battered face and his filthy, torn and blood-stained suit, and forced himself out into the hot and constant wind, his head was swimming again. Still, he made his way along the beach and slowly up the stairs, and into the piazza. The piazza was empty, and before all the windows the shutters were closed. A torn and dirty piece of paper was caught up

85

by a gust of wind and brushed against his cheek. He opened the door of the post office.

The dusty, dreary room was deserted, and Charles had to wait for some minutes before the ugly face of the postmistress appeared in the little window. He could hear some sort of a machine clicking out Morse code into an apparently unheeding world. He asked for four cable forms. The postmistress counted them out very carefully, checking again to make sure that she had not given him one too many. She did not say a word as she thrust them through the hatch, slamming the little window shut as soon as she had done so. Charles took them across to a chest-high ledge, to which were chained a pen and a bottle of purple ink.

He thought out carefully what he would say, and he wrote as legibly as he could with the nasty nib. He sent one cable to his wife, one to his partner and one to his bank, asking each to forward him a thousand dollars immediately. One of these, at least, should get through in a comprehensible form, he decided. And once he had some money, he would not be trapped in this frightening place. Then he wrote out a telegram to the American consulate.

AM AMERICAN CITIZEN STRANDED IN SIANO MONEY STOLEN SERIOUS TROUBLE CAN YOU COME OR SEND REPRESENTATIVE URGENTEST CHARLES WARREN.

He read it through and crossed out the words "MONEY STOLEN." That was irrelevant. Except that, since he must send the telegram collect, perhaps he should explain why he was asking the consulate to pay for it. He wrote in the deleted words again. Then he knocked on the window of frosted glass. For a little time there was no sound save the irregular ticking of the machine. Suddenly the glass

86

opened, and the face was there, the great mole on the side of her nose only a few inches from his eyes. He drew back and passed her the forms. He began to speak, but the head in the window moved from side to side. She handed back to him the telegram to the consul, saying something quickly in a deep, harsh voice. He did not understand, and testily, with an ink-stained finger, she pointed at the crossed out words. She pushed another form towards him and closed the glass window.

He wrote it out again, and again had to wait before the window was opened. Now he noticed that the church bell was tolling very slowly. She counted the words of each cable twice, and then consulted a great ledger, running her dirty finger up and down long columns of figures. She wrote something in pencil on each form; on another piece of paper she did a lengthy calculation. Finally she said, without looking up:

"*Ottomila trecento quarantacinque lire.*"

Charles had thought out what he had to say. Speaking clearly, he said:

"*Addressato pagare. Non io. Pagare New York.*"

Now she glanced up and repeated, tapping her pencil against the counter:

"*Ottomila trecento quarantacinque lire.*"

Charles possessed exactly seventy lire. Eight thousand, three hundred and forty-five was something less than twenty-five dollars. She might as well have asked him for a million. Once again, laboriously, he began his explanation. The church bell was tolling a little more rapidly now, and Charles began to feel a mounting desperation as he first explained and then beseeched the unmoving face in the window. Suddenly the woman spoke, very quickly, and slammed shut the window.

Charles was shouting now, and he banged at the

window with his fist. For a moment he feared he was
going to burst into tears. Then, at the far end of the
counter, a door opened and the postmistress appeared.
Her face in the window had been so big, and her power
over him as she slammed the window so total, that
he had thought of her as larger than lifesize, a monu-
mental and malignant principality. Yet the woman in
the black dress was only some four feet tall, a sort of
freak with her distended head. She held in her hand a
great bunch of heavy keys, and she pointed to the door.
He tried now to propitiate this evil power, talking, gesturing, grimacing. But she merely pointed, advancing on
him. He backed away from her, still talking, and soon
was out in the piazza, where there were now many
people. She did not answer. He was still talking as she
shut and locked the door of the post office. Then, without
a word, she turned and walked away. He would have
shouted, run after her, his useless telegrams clutched in
his hand. But he was conscious that the people were
staring at him, and from them there seemed to emanate
a sort of hissing noise. He stopped and looked about him.
And now he understood where he was. Up the steps,
from the beach, there came the funeral procession, walking slowly, almost in time to the tolling of the bell. The
people in the piazza stood in total silence. Charles,
stepping back into the doorway of the post office, tried
to obliterate himself in the small shadow that the lintel
cast. He raised his fist to his bruised lips.

In Italy the authorities recognize the exacerbating
effect of that monotonous hot wind, which usually blows
itself out after three days: it is an acceptable excuse in
a court of law and one that will cause a southern judge to
mitigate his punishment for a crime of violence com-
mitted at such a time. This Charles did not know, but he

could not avoid feeling the massive hatred that existed against him among the men and women grouped in the piazza, and he was very frightened. He was more than frightened. He had had little sleep the previous night. His body was staggered by the beating that had been administered to it, yesterday evening. He had eaten nothing in twenty-four hours. And now he was confronted with this wall of detestation. As he pressed himself against the door of the post office, it did not matter that he had not killed little Luigi, that he had in fact been attempting to save the child pain. By his actions he had caused the emotions that surrounded him to come into existence, and thus his fear was a guilty fear, the fear of guilt.

Slowly the little procession wound around the piazza; one of the four men carrying the child's coffin was Mario. The sobs of the mother as she walked behind were clearly audible in the silence. It was almost from this spot that Charles, with Concetta beside him, had watched that other procession, so few days ago. But now it was at him, he was sure, that they were all staring. Everywhere there were eyes, against the green-tiled dome of the church, in the pink and white and pale-blue walls of the houses, behind the shuttered windows, eyes among the waves of sound from the slow-moving bell and in the tormenting wind. The procession moved past him, and each person's eyes were fixed on him. From each of the mourners, as from each of the spectators, there came the same cruel message. And Charles had now a hysterical certainty that unless, somehow, he escaped from Siano he would be killed. Even through the doors of the church, from within its candle-studded darkness, he thought to see the eyes of the priest looking coldly into his.

And then the funeral procession had passed up the

steps and was gone. The shutters were being reopened, and Charles's spasm of terror had passed. Yet he knew now that he must, somehow, regain contact with the outside world, with what he still thought of as the real world. He would even humiliate himself to the extent of asking for Adelmo's help. The crowd in the piazza was dispersing, and nobody looked at him as he made his way to the stairs.

The café was half full when he entered it, the men talking in low, solemn voices. They took no notice of him as he walked between the tables to the far end where Adelmo was standing, his arms folded.

"Adelmo . . ." he began.

"Why you come here? We don't want you here. Get out."

"Adelmo, can I . . . will you lend me the money to send some telegrams?"

Adelmo laughed briefly and spat. Charles had really expected nothing else. There was only one more hope.

"Adelmo, will you, would you let me use your telephone to ring the American consulate in Naples?"

The innkeeper studied the battered, pleading face for a moment. The men were all watching the interchange between them. Perhaps it was for this reason, or perhaps Adelmo felt some shame for what he had done the night before; in any case, at last he shrugged his shoulders.

"O.K."

"Adelmo, thank you. And Adelmo, would you please ask for the number for me?"

The innkeeper raised his eyebrows. Then he turned away. Charles watched him pick the earpiece off its hook, turn the handle at the side of the machine, and heard him ask the operator for the American consulate. Adelmo waited, with his back to him, and Charles waited and

90

behind him the men in the café waited too. Charles did not wish to look at them. He still had a little pride left.

Adelmo said something into the mouthpiece, then hung up and came back into the bar. He said:

"The girl say there's a delay to Naples. She ring back."

Charles had thought this link, too, was broken. Now he felt a sudden rebirth of hope. He said:

"Do you mind if I wait here?"

"Wait outside."

"Yes . . . and, thank you, Adelmo."

Adelmo said nothing. Charles went out through the metallic curtain into the wind and the glare. He waited for perhaps half an hour, perhaps an hour. It was impossible to say. After a little time he saw the people coming back from the funeral. Some of the men, in black clothes, walked past him into the café. The sound of the talk from in there was heavy and monotonous. He watched the waves breaking sluggishly along the sand until the monotony of the repeated pattern made him fear he might faint. He worked out, over and over again, what he must tell the consul. He must make his voice sound clear and sure, the whole business a stupid misunderstanding. He would speak as one American gentleman to another, and the consul would surely get into his car at once and come out here. It would not take him more than an hour in his Buick or Chrysler. Could he imply that he was frightened for his life? Perhaps, perhaps not, it would depend on what sort of a man the consul turned out to be. He ran through the conversation again. He was not aware that on the balcony above the old man was watching. The old man could even distinguish the words that Charles, unconsciously, spoke aloud as he rehearsed his conversation. He did not, of course, understand them.

The sun reached and passed its zenith. Occasionally a man would go into or come out of the café. Charles had repeated his future conversation until the words had become almost meaningless to him. He looked along the beach again, up at the English tower outlined against the sky. Did Concetta know of his agony? Surely she would have helped him by now, had she known. Or perhaps not. Perhaps she hated him too. He looked the other way. A man was emerging at the bottom on the steps, a man wearing an open-necked shirt, a blond, tall man whom Charles had never seen before, a stranger with a book in his hand. At that moment the telephone rang inside the café and Charles jumped to his feet. He pushed through the curtain. Adelmo was beckoning him to the telephone.

"Hello, is that the American consulate?"

"Pronto!" It was a female voice.

"Hello, I want to speak to the consul."

"Pronto!"

"Hello, can you hear me?"

"Chi parla?"

"Hello, is that the American consulate?"

"Consolato Americano."

At least he was through to the right number.

"I want to speak to the consul."

"Chi parla?"

The voice was toneless and inhuman.

"Please get me someone who speaks English."

"Prego?"

"The consul. Give me the consul."

"Chi parla?"

He turned away from the phone.

"Adelmo, please, can you help me?"

Adelmo took the earpiece from him and said some-

92

thing before handing it back. The girl was there again. She said:

"Pronto!"

"I want the consul."

"Chi parla?"

Adelmo said:

"She ask who you are."

"Warren," he shouted into the phone, which was beginning to emit crackling noises, "Charles Warren."

"Prego?"

He repeated his name. At last she seemed to understand, for he heard her moving her receiver up and down at the far end, twenty miles away in Naples. There was silence. Charles had just decided that he had been cut off, when he heard, very faintly, a man's voice:

"Pronto!"

"Hello, is that the American consul?"

"Prego?"

The crackling had grown louder.

"Are you the consul?" he bawled.

"Chi parla?"

"Can you speak English?"

Suddenly the voice was much louder. In a strong Italian accent the man said:

"Yes, I spik English. Who you want?"

"I want to talk to the American consul."

"Who you?"

"My name is Warren, Charles Warren."

"Who?"

"Warren. Double-u, a, double r, e, n."

"Please?"

Charles spelled his name out several times before the man got it.

"What you want?"

"I want to speak to the consul."

"You want to speak the consul? Why?"

"I'm an American citizen, and I'm in trouble. I must speak to the consul."

"State the nature of your business."

"Please connect me with the consul."

"The consul not here. The consul out to lunch."

"Oh, God!"

"Prego?"

"Hello! Is there a vice-consul?"

"The vice-consul gone out to lunch."

There was a sudden babble of voices over the line. Then it was clear again.

"Hello!"

The man's voice was extremely weak and remote once again. Charles shouted.

"When will the consul be back? WHEN WILL HE BE BACK?"

"Monday. You better phone again Monday. Hello? Hello? You hear me? Tomorrow Saturday, he not here. You phone again Monday. You hear me? Monday!"

There was a crackling noise over the wire.

"Hello," said Charles.

"Pronto!" It was the voice of the girl to whom he had first spoken.

"Pronto! Pronto!"

Then even that voice disappeared in a rush of meaningless sound, and the telephone went dead. Charles slowly replaced the earpiece on its hook. He walked through the café and out on to the terrace. The yellow-haired man was seated at one of the tables, reading his book.

Chapter Four

IT WAS the blue packet of English cigarettes on the man's table that he first noticed. The longing to smoke was urgent and irresistible. He reached into his pocket, but remembered at once that he had smoked his last cigarette during his long vigil of the night before. Almost at once, though, he realized the secondary and far greater significance of the *Player's Navy Cut*. The man had not stopped reading; a small glass of vermouth was before him. Charles cleared his throat. The man glanced up, frowned, and went back to his book. Charles said:

"Are you an Englishman?"

Now the man closed his book, keeping his middle finger between the pages to mark his place. His face was yellowish. He might have been some forty years old, but his age was hard to guess precisely, since his skin had the unnatural smoothness of certain ageless women whose faces have been lifted. His blond hair, which he wore rather long, was most carefully arranged in waves or curls which even the south wind had not disturbed. His eyes were of a cold and watery blue and there were red pimples about his mouth and on his throat. He held his head far back he as replied, enunciating very carefully in his deliberate Oxford accent:

"I am."

There was no invitation either in the voice or in his manner, as he looked Charles up and down, observing his torn, stained suit, his cut face, his trembling hands. Indeed his expression was rather one of distaste. But this Charles hardly noticed.

"Thank God!" he said. "You can't imagine what a miracle it is that you should have turned up here today. You can't begin to imagine . . ."

"Really?" remarked the Englishman, still not removing his finger from between the pages of the book.

Charles had sat down across the table from him.

"Are you staying here?" he asked.

"No. If it's any concern of yours, I took the wrong road. I am on my way to Positano. I am leaving immediately after I have had my luncheon."

"You've got a car?"

"Really, you are very inquisitive, if I may say so. Yes, since you ask, I motored here."

"Then you could take me with you?"

"Take you with me? What an extraordinary idea!"

"Listen, let me tell you what's happened. I'm in the most appalling trouble. I . . . Could I have one of your cigarettes? I haven't got any left."

"Well . . ." said the Englishman, and frowned. Then he offered Charles the packet, took one himself, lit them both with a cheap tin cigarette lighter, and replaced packet and lighter in the pocket of his gray flannel trousers.

"Thank you. Please let me tell you what has happened. I'm certain you'll help me."

The Englishman sighed and sipped the little glass of vermouth before him. His expression was primarily one of irritation at being thus disturbed. It became only slightly modified by disgust as Charles, hastily and clumsily, told the story of Concetta, of his beating-up, of the dead child, of his fear. At last his voice trailed away.

The Englishman said nothing. Charles would have liked to ask for another cigarette, but did not dare. Still the Englishman did not speak. At last Charles said:

"So you see you've got to help me get out of here."

"Got to, little man, got to? That is no way to speak to princes or benefactors."

"What's that?"

"Merely a semi-quotation from Queen Elizabeth."

"I'm sorry, I didn't mean to . . ."

"I daresay not. You say you are supposed to be a doctor? You don't look like a doctor."

"I know I don't. But then you wouldn't either if you'd been beaten up like I was."

"My dear sir, I would make quite certain that I wasn't, as you put it, beaten up in such a fashion."

"Will you take me with you this afternoon?"

The Englishman thrust his chin even higher. Then, reaching into his trouser pocket, he took out his cigarettes. He did not offer Charles one. Before replying he took a long draw and puffed out a great cloud of gray tobacco smoke.

"No," he said, "I shall not."

"But, don't you see, they're likely to kill me, they . . ."

He fell silent. Adelmo had appeared through the metal curtain. The Englishman spoke to him in fluent Italian. When Adelmo had gone back into the café, the Englishman said:

"You are being hysterical, a national characteristic of Americans, I'm told. Just because these people don't have deep freeze units and, er, television sets, you are quite wrong to suppose that they are any less civilized than your compatriots. Indeed, one might say, quite the contrary."

"Look at my face. You see what they did to me last night. I tell you . . ."

The Englishman was looking at his face. He blew out another cloud of smoke. He said:

"You come to this little fishing village. You seduce one of the girls. And you are surprised that they don't all applaud you because you represent the dollar sign. Just think what would happen to a Negro in the United States in similar circumstances, and then perhaps you will feel a little less sorry for yourself."

Adelmo had come out while the Englishman was talking. He had refilled his glass, a slight smile playing about his lips, and had gone back inside.

"Besides," the Englishman went on, "from what you have told me, though I must say I found your story a little hard to follow, you are under some sort of arrest in connection with the death of this child. Am I not correct?"

"But I explained to you . . ."

"Exactly. You apparently think that it is quite in order for anybody who calls himself a doctor to administer noxious drugs to peasants, to make them ignore the advice of their physician, and then, when a person dies as a result of his bungling interference, to run away. And now you would like to involve me in your troubles. To make me, in fact, an accomplice. But that wouldn't suit me, it wouldn't suit me at all. You see, I have a certain respect for Italy and the Italians, which is no doubt incomprehensible to you. I have no desire to break their laws or to help anyone else to do so. But then, of course, I am a European, and we see these things somewhat differently."

Charles felt himself sagging. He was hardly listening to what the man was saying, and was both fascinated and

98

disgusted by the pimples on the throat that arose from the open green cotton shirt.

"You won't take me with you, then?"

"Really, you seem to be quite remarkably dense. Have you not understood a word I said?"

"Oh, yes, I understand well enough." Charles fell silent. The Englishman stubbed out his cigarette and pulled his book toward him. Charles said:

"Can you lend me some money?"

"Money? No, certainly not."

"Can you lend me the price of a few cables? You'll get it back within two or three days. I promise you."

"I have no money to spare. No doubt you are unaware that in England there is something called a dollar crisis. We English are only allowed to take the sum of twenty-five pounds abroad with us. This does not allow us to indulge in quixotic acts of charity to strangers encountered in seaside cafés."

"I'm not asking for charity. I'm asking you for a small loan. Surely ten thousand lire would make no difference to you over a period of two or three days?"

"Whether it would or not is quite beside the point. This coast, my dear sir, is littered with spongers trying to get money from tourists. And now, if you will be so good, I should like to return to my book. Besides, if you lack the money to send telegrams, you can always write a letter. We do, in Europe, you know."

Adelmo had come out on the terrace again. It was plain to him that Charles was annoying the Englishman. He moved across. Charles saw the expression on his face, and said hastily:

"If I wrote a letter, would you post it for me? I don't know if it would go from here. I think they'd intercept it."

The Englishman laughed, a high, homosexual laugh. "My dear sir, you *are* hysterical!"

Adelmo now said, in English:

"Is this man annoying you?"

The Englishman turned to Adelmo and smiled:

"He is rather, but I think he is going now." Then, turning back to Charles: "Yes, you really are hysterical. But to humor you, or rather to get rid of you—all right. If you wish to write a letter, I'll post it for you. I'll even go so far as to buy the stamp. There now! But you had better bring it to me here within the hour. Does that satisfy you?" And then, to Adelmo: "I should like one more glass of your excellent vermouth and my luncheon."

Charles got up and walked down the steps of the café terrace. Behind him he heard the Englishman speaking in Italian to Adelmo, and then they both laughed. His legs felt very weak as he made his way through the loose sand toward his room.

It took him a long time to write the letter, which he had decided he would address to the American ambassador in Rome. His mind kept going blank, and he would sit for several minutes staring through the window, counting the waves as they ran up the sand or watching the swoopings of a gull in a vacant reverie. Then, when he began to write again, sudden stabs of pain in his right shoulder would break his train of thought and he would have to make an effort to remember what it was that he was attempting to say to this distant and improbable person for whom the letter was destined. *Dear Sir* or perhaps it should be *Dear Mr. Ambassador,* and, later on, *I am not hysterical, but I know that these people will kill me,* and then a long passage about his inability to communicate with the outside world. *I am a doctor by profession, I was only trying to do what I could for the child, who in*

100

any case was dying. The letter went on and on, until at last: *Unless you can help me at once I don't know what will happen.* He read it through, frowning as he did so, forcing himself to concentrate on the meaning of each word. He had not mentioned Concetta, and he was glad he had not done so. He thought it was quite right, clever even, that he had not brought her in. In the first place, it might lose him the sympathy of the faceless ambassador to whom he was writing, though as one man to another the ambassador would probably have understood. Should it go in as a postscript? He gazed out of the window. The sun seemed brighter. Perhaps the wind was dropping? He listened attentively. No, he could still hear it, soughing over the sand. And the dog was barking too. Funny he hadn't heard it before. He shook his head and forced his eyes back to the letter he had written . . . *an old man who obviously did not know what he was doing, or else of course I should never have intervened.* What was it that he had been wondering about? Oh yes, Concetta. No, he was quite right to leave her out. The letter was too long already. Would the ambassador read it to the end? But surely he must? What did they do all day long, ambassadors? Signing things in ornate rooms with gold fountain pens, among the flash of cameramen's bulbs. It was some newsreel that he had seen a long time ago, a group of men seated at an enormous table, each signing his name very quickly, and then turning and smiling at the others. But he didn't think they had been ambassadors. He must hurry up and address the envelope. *The American Ambassador, Rome, Italy.* It did not look right. He took another envelope, moving his arm too quickly, so that pain pierced his shoulder. *The Ambassador, The United States Embassy,* ROMA. No need to put Italy. And at the top he wrote: *Personal and Very Urgent.*

He folded the sheet of paper, put it into the envelope and licked the strip of gum along the flap. Half a dozen times he ran his thumb along the join, for he was afraid that it might come open and the letter drop out. He wrote his name and address carefully on the back flap. And now he must take it to the Englishman. Then he would have done all he had to do, he would have completed his duties, he would be free to stare at the sea. The howling of the dog was rather like an air raid siren. Poor dog.

The knock on the door scarcely roused him from his lethargy.

"Come in," he said automatically and unnecessarily. The policeman had already opened the door and was saying something, gesturing Charles to come with him. Charles picked up his letter and followed him outside.

It was the younger policeman, a heavily built and swarthy man with a small black mustache. He did not look at Charles, who was walking beside him, nor did he even glance at the three fishermen who stared from beside their boats. This official impassively was, somehow, an encouragement and relief to Charles. He was in the hands of the authorities, as he might have been in the army or even back at school. And the authorities, though usually callous and sometimes fickle or stupid, were not cruel. Therefore he could surrender himself to their jurisdiction, whether it were to prison that they were planning now to send him or whether it was merely to be an interview. For a little time at least the burden of decision was lifted from him. Besides, his letter was written.

And then he realized that they had passed the café. He looked back. The Englishman was still seated on the terrace, immersed in his book. Charles would have liked to run back and give him the letter, but the policeman,

102

who had stopped when Charles did, was clearly impatient to move on. Nor did Charles wish to break their silent and reassuring relationship by an attempted explanation. He walked up the stairs with him.

It was to the mayor's office that the policeman led him. Charles even attempted a smile as he came in, but it remained unanswered. The mayor was seated behind his desk, his elbows resting upon its edge, and he kept bringing his finger-tips together with a little sound like a flabby pendulum. To his left, and slightly behind him, stood the other policeman, the *maresciallo,* while to his right was the aged doctor, seated in the pink armchair. The policeman who had accompanied Charles said something and withdrew out of sight, behind Charles. For perhaps a whole minute the mayor's small eyes in the fat and greasy face were fixed on Charles. Then he turned to the doctor and spoke. The old man said, in his slow but comprehensible French:

"The police authorities of the provincial capital must be informed concerning the death of the infant, Luigi Spinta. Since you delivered the poisonous drugs of which the child died, it is necessary to ask you a number of questions. It will then be decided, by the provincial authorities, whether you are to be prosecuted on a charge of manslaughter, or whether your offense has merely been that of practicing medicine in Italy without a permit."

Charles said nothing, and the old man exchanged a few words with the mayor. The latter was glancing at a form that lay before him on his desk, and which Charles recognized as being the residence permit which he had filled upon the day of his arrival.

"You give your profession as a doctor," said the old man. "What sort of doctor are you supposed to be?"

"A diagnostician," answered Charles. The word, in French, sounded odd.

"What?"

Charles repeated it. The old man said:

"You do not understand. You give your profession as doctor. You are not a doctor of music, perhaps, or a doctor of divinity? You are a doctor of medicine?"

"Oh, yes."

"You have a medical degree?"

"Yes, of course."

"Ah, and from what university do you hold this degree?"

Charles told him.

The old man repeated it to the mayor, who nodded solemnly. The old man wrote it down, but had trouble with the spelling. Charles tried to help; the old man waved him angrily away. Charles resigned himself again to their will.

"This degree is recognized in the United States as entitling you to practice medicine?"

"Yes, certainly."

"Have you proof that you hold this degree? Have you, for example, a diploma?"

The mayor's finger-tips kept coming together and parting again. And Charles felt a sudden inclination to smile, though he could not have said why. He mastered it.

"Yes, but not with me." He added: "But I imagine you could check up on me through the medical registers."

"Ah," said the old man, and repeated this to the mayor. Then he said:

"The mayor wishes to know what proof you can produce that you are in fact a doctor."

Charles said:

"Why, none. Except . . ."

104

"What proof can you produce that your name is in fact Charles Warren? The mayor says that he has reason to believe that your name is Warner."

Charles remembered the letter from the Express Company. It was really all so silly, so remote. He felt as though he were watching this scene from some incredible distance. Yet he had no thought but to be as helpful as possible to these beetles in their quest.

"I think I have my driving license, and one or two other documents."

He took out his pocket book. There were three papers in it that carried his name, including his army discharge form. This, since it bore a fingerprint, should, he thought, satisfy the Italian. He handed them to the old doctor who immediately passed them to the mayor. For some little time the mayor pondered them in silence. Then he spoke to the old man. The man said:

"The mayor wants to know why, if you are a doctor, this document says that you are a soldier, a major."

Charles explained. He even leaned across and pointed to the relevant part of the sheet of paper, where he was described as a doctor, a member of the Army Medical Corps. The mayor nodded heavily. The old man said:

"So you are an army doctor? Why did you not say so before? Do you have your leave papers?"

Laboriously Charles explained again. But he saw that the old man wrote down that he was an army doctor. The various documents were handed back to him, and he put them away in his pocket book. The old man said:

"It is understood that you are a doctor. Do you have a permit to practice in Italy?"

"No."

"You are aware that no foreign doctor may practice in

Italy without a permit? You do not perhaps have such a regulation in America?"

"I have no intention of practicing in Italy. I'm here on a holiday." A holiday! he thought.

The old man repeated this to the mayor. The latter said something and the old man now asked:

"What is your mother's maiden name, her place and date of birth?"

"Her name was Ann Sellars. She was born, I think, in Vermont, about 1886. I am not sure of this."

"You are not sure? Very well, we will come back to that later."

The mayor said something impatiently. The old doctor asked:

"When did you deliver these poisonous drugs to the child, Luigi Spinta?"

"I gave him two sleeping pills at about eight o'clock last night."

"Two? Two only?"

"Yes, two."

"And what do these pills contain?"

He had taken the box from the mayor, who had apparently been holding it on his lap. Charles said:

"They have a sodium-amytal base, about a grain of it, I think. I am not quite sure. The formula is given on the lid."

"Exactly," said the old man. "And two pills is not enough."

"Not enough?"

"Two pills would not comprise a lethal dose. I suspect that you administered a considerably larger dose to the child."

Charles hesitated:

106

"I left the box behind. Perhaps the parents gave him more of the pills later."

The doctor translated. Then he said:

"You are accusing Antonio and Maria Spinta of having administered the poisonous drugs?"

"No, no. I merely meant . . ."

"How many pills did you give the child?"

"Two."

"And how many were there left in the box?"

"I am not sure. Perhaps eight or ten."

"Eight or ten. I see. That would indeed be a lethal dose for a small child."

There was a short colloquy between the doctor and the mayor. The latter nodded several times, before saying to Charles:

"Why did you give the child these drugs, two or ten as the case may be?"

"Because the child was in great pain, I wished to save him pain."

"You were practicing euthanasia?"

Charles felt extraordinarily tired, now, and had absolutely no wish to smile.

"No, no. I merely wished to anaesthetize the child, while I telephoned you."

The doctor raised his eyebrows at this and spoke quickly to the mayor.

"You wished to telephone me? Why did you not do so?"

Charles fell silent. The doctor went on:

"It is understood that last night you were drunk and attempted to fight the owner of the café on the beach. Was this before or after you intended to telephone me, as it was your duty to do?"

107

"I was not drunk. I attempted to telephone you. Adelmo would not let me."

The doctor repeated this to the mayor, who shrugged his shoulders. The doctor said:

"That is a statement which will be checked. It does not correspond with what has so far been said by other witnesses."

Charles did not speak. The old man went on:

"Meanwhile, you had left the other pills with the parents? Is that what you maintain?"

"Yes."

"Had you warned them that these pills were dangerous?"

"No, I don't think so. I intended to go back, after I had telephoned you."

"But you did not telephone me and you did not go back. You left these dangerous pills in the hands of two ignorant peasants, after having first shown them how to administer them to the child. Would you say that that was in accordance with the ethics of the medical profession? Would you do such a thing in America?"

In a low voice, Charles said:

"No."

"And now you accuse Antonio and Maria Spinta of having poisoned their own child? You do not think that you are responsible for the child's death?"

For the first time Charles realized that the old man was enjoying this cross-examination, and the realization made his blood freeze. Slowly he said:

"Doctor, the child had meningitis." He realized from the expression of anger on the old man's face, that he had said exactly the wrong thing. He went on: "Perhaps I did wrong in law to give the child the two pills. I am sure that I was morally right, though. It was wrong of me to leave the box behind. But then I could hardly expect that I would be beaten unconscious while trying to telephone you. Can you not see that it was all an accident?"

The doctor translated this at length to the mayor, who nodded and spoke slowly. Then the doctor said:

"We now have your version of the events that led up to the death of the child. The facts will be forwarded to the provincial authorities who will decide what steps should be taken. And now you must fill up this form."

It was a long form, and it caused Charles some trouble. The mayor and the doctor talked while he was doing this, and once the mayor laughed, briefly. During all this interview the two carabinieri had stood motionless, only occasionally shifting their weight from foot to foot.

At last Charles had finished. He straightened up, and glanced out of the window. Walking across the piazza, toward the steps that led to the upper road, was the Englishman. Quickly Charles said to the doctor:

"There is a man out there. I must speak to him."

"Where? What man? What do you mean?"

Charles had moved toward the door, but the policeman blocked his way. The mayor said something in a very loud voice, and Charles stopped. The mayor spoke to the doctor, who now said:

"The mayor wishes you to understand that you are in the position of a prisoner. It is only by his charity that you are not at this moment in prison. You will not leave this room until you have received his instructions."

"But I must see that man . . . I must see that man . . ."

Nobody answered him. The mayor was reading through the completed form. After what seemed an interminable silence he replaced it on the desk before him, brought his fingertips together again, and began to speak. When he had done the doctor said:

"The mayor wishes you to know that he will await instructions from the provincial authorities as to what shall be done in the case of the Spinta child deceased, and what charges, if any, are to be preferred against you. It may interest you to know that I have suggested that your offense is only one of criminal negligence, and have suggested that a report forwarded through the Italian medical authorities to the medical authorities of the United States would be the suitable action to take. However, by practicing in Italy you have broken the civil law. That is a matter for the police. Whether or not they will prosecute remains to be seen. Do you understand?"

Charles had hardly listened. The Englishman was out of sight. He had been walking slowly. How long would it take him to get to the top?

"Do you understand?"

"Yes, yes. Can I go now?"

"Meanwhile there is a second charge against you, to wit, a civil case involving debts to various persons in the community of Siano. Unless these debts are settled forthwith a writ or writs will be served upon you. Do you understand?"

"Yes, just as soon as my money arrives. Please, can I go now?"

"The mayor wishes you to know that you are not authorized to leave Siano until these matters have been decided, that is to say until he has heard the decision of the provincial authorities concerning your complicity in the death of the child Luigi Spinta, and until the debts that you have contracted in Siano have been paid in full. Do you understand?"

"Yes, I understand. Is that all?"

110

The doctor spoke to the mayor, who answered. The doctor said:

"That is all. You are not to attempt to leave Siano. You may go now."

The policeman stepped aside. Charles hurried through the door and down the stairs. His side was beginning once again to ache as he ran across the piazza, nearly colliding with an old woman. He thought he might just catch up with the Englishman. From the bottom of the steps he could see about two thirds of the way up. There the long flight turned a corner, and the road at the top was out of sight. The Englishman must have passed the bend, for Charles could not see him. He began to run up the steps.

Chapter Five

HIS BREATH was coming in great, searing gasps as he forced himself up the last few steps that led to the road. He could hear the engine of the car starting.

"Stop!" he cried, "Stop!" But only a feeble sound passed his lips, and even that was blown away by the hot and steady wind. He could just see, above the line of wall, the hard, black roof of the car as it moved off toward the tunnel.

He reached the top and lurched into the middle of the earthen road. The car was now almost at the tunnel's mouth. He waved his arms:

"Stop! Stop!"

The car moved on, and he ran a few steps after it. Surely the man must look back or glance into his mirror? The car disappeared into the darkness of the tunnel. Charles stood still, in the center of the roadway. Once the Englishman must have applied his brakes, for a red light glowed far down the tunnel, and Charles was convinced that he had seen him, that he was coming back. The light vanished. For a second the car was silhouetted against the distant mouth of the tunnel. Then it was gone forever, and the semicircle of light at the far end, no bigger, it seemed, than the moon at the base of his little fingernail, was unobstructed. Charles moved across to the wall and buried his head in his arms. He would have liked to sob out his rage and mortification and misery, but even this he could not do.

Gradually the pain in his side lessened. He lifted his head. The wind hummed through the telegraph wires that flanked the road. Far below, on the beach, he could see tiny people moving. Were they going to his room, were they looking for him? He tried to follow their movements, to discern the intentions of those distant spots, but his eyes kept losing them in the afternoon haze of heat. Perhaps, after all, those black dots only existed on his own retina. And then, suddenly, he realized that he was alone up here.

He was absolutely alone. Quickly he looked all about him. There was no sound save for the wind in the wires. Up above, the brownish-yellow hillside was deserted. Nobody had followed him up the steps. He had almost escaped from Siano.

Normally he could easily have walked twenty miles. Now his head was swimming, and the sweat of his body had soaked right through his torn, stained flannel suit. Also there was the pain in his side, though that had almost gone. But if he went back down . . . It was now more than twenty-four hours since last he had eaten. But if he went back down . . . Suppose he walked, at once, three miles. Could he manage three miles? He thought so. Then he might find some shady place in which to sleep until nightfall. And when the sun rose again, who could tell how far he might have gone? Suppose, for instance, that a car passed? He could stop it and ask for a lift. No, for the car would be coming from Siano. But by morning he might have reached another village. There had been several villages on the way out. He could not remember how far from Siano they had been. But if he went back down . . .

He looked about him once again. Nobody, so far as the eyes could see, no one, no sound save the wind. Stealthily, almost, he set off toward the tunnel. By its mouth he stopped and looked back. No, he was not being followed. He entered the tunnel.

It was nearly half a mile long, a triumph of fascist engineering, although an uncompleted one. The walls were rough, damp with moisture when he touched them with his outstretched hand. It was a low tunnel, and soon he was in deep shadow. Blacker shadows were cast by great lump-like pieces of rock that stuck out from its coarse sides.

At first the cool darkness of the tunnel was a relief after the garish glare from which he had come, but as he penetrated farther toward its dank center, the dimness and the weight of stone began to fill him with an unreasoning fear. He realized that he was whispering aloud:

"I am not a coward. I am not running away from what I did. It is those others. I have always been a brave man, a decent man. I must save my life. Every man must save his life if he can." He was walking more slowly now. "I

113

must go on. It would be suicide to go back. That is what is cowardly, suicide. I am not a coward. I am afraid of the people back there. I am not frightened by this tunnel. See, I am not afraid. I am walking on. And, later, when I am back home, in my own home . . . WHAT'S THAT?"

Far ahead of him he could hear footsteps, and the sound of tuneless whistling. He pressed himself against the buttress of rock. The footsteps and the whistling drew closer. Charles felt the dampness of the tunnel's wall against the nape of his neck and the palms of his hands. He could make out the approaching figure now. It was a man, and he walked past without seeing Charles, whistling all the time. But something touched the calf of his leg. Charles almost screamed. Then the man, who was twenty yards on, whistled two clear notes, and the little dog ran after him. Gradually Charles stopped trembling. He saw the man and the dog emerge at the far end of the tunnel, two or three hundred yards away. Slowly Charles went on, almost tiptoeing now.

"Why have they let me escape like this? When will they start hunting me? They must know by now that I have gone. They'll be armed. Will the consul in Naples believe me? Would Betty believe me? Concetta would believe me, she would know it was an accident . . . about the child. They all know that it was an accident. I was only doing what was right. Everyone must know that. They know. That's why they will kill me. Because they know I am innocent. They hate me and they know I am innocent and therefore they will murder me. But I won't die. I'll escape, now, I am escaping, yard by yard, breath by breath, step by step, pain by pain. See, I am nearly a third of the way down the tunnel already. It is almost pitch dark. I am not afraid of the dark. I am not a coward. WHAT'S THAT?"

114

The end of the tunnel toward which he was walking was filled with shadows, and there was the sound of many, hurrying feet. Charles stopped, petrified. Now that they had entered the tunnel, he could not see them, but he could hear them, the noise reverberating to fill the tunnel.

"It was all a trick. They knew all the time. They were waiting for me there. That's why they didn't follow me. Oh God, what shall I do?"

The noise of the many footsteps grew louder and louder, but there was no word spoken.

"Oh God, they are coming in silence to murder me in this dark tunnel. Oh God, help me."

And now he could move his muscles again. He turned and ran, stumbling and panting, back the way that he had come. The noise of the following footsteps was like thunder in his ears, like the roll of drums, the beating of surf, the terrible tattoo of the Furies. He ran, and they ran after, until at last he burst out into the glaring sunshine. He could go no further. There was a heap of gravel that the workmen had left behind, these many years ago. Onto this Charles threw himself, and waited for his murderers. At least he would die in the sunlight.

At last they came out of the tunnel's mouth, perhaps a dozen goats, driven by an old woman. As they passed, each goat looked at him, from its weird black eyes with the satanic yellow stripe down the center. Each evil face was full of mocking curiosity as the ill-smelling beasts stared at the man who had so unaccountably run away. Then, with a toss of their oblong, bearded heads, they trotted on. The old woman nodded too, and they were gone.

For a long time Charles sat down on the heap of gravel. Now he knew he could not re-enter the tunnel.

But would God let him die like this? God is a just God. If only he could pray.

"Oh, God . . ." he prayed, "Oh, God . . ."

It was no prayer. It was just two words from nothing to nothing. How many years was it since he had prayed? Had he ever done so, save as a small child kneeling against the edge of his bed beside his mother's knee? He did not know how to pray. Or he had forgotten.

And then Charles thought of the priest. He got up and began slowly to descend the four hundred and twenty-seven steps that led down into Siano. Down there the green dome of the church rose up, unmoved in many hundred years. It was there that he must go.

Although he had often meant to visit the church of Siano, he had never before done so. It was a light place, the walls a faded, yellowish white as were the two rows of ornate, plaster pillars that flanked the nave, and it was surprisingly large for a village the size of Siano. The windows were high up on either side, and the glass was unstained, so that all the tawdry tinsel of its furnishings immediately filled Charles's eye. Above the high altar, before which there was a railing and stained red carpeting, there hung a huge picture in a twisting, gilded frame, a flabby and simpering Madonna holding in her arms an Infant Jesus who had the features of a self-satisfied, middle-aged business man. To the left of this altar was another, which contained the great painted bust of the patron saint. Above the altar on the other side was a picture of the Sacred Heart, a terribly realistic, spongy mass of bleeding tissue among what seemed to be rays of silver and gold paper. There were side chapels, each containing its own brilliant bric-à-brac, statues dressed up like dolls in faded clothing, pictures of writhing

116

martyrs, convoluted candlesticks, memorial plaques surmounted by bas-reliefs, the lettering very black against
the white marble, bunches of flowers jammed higgle-
dipiggledy into bronze or silver vases of complicated
design. In a stand such as one sees outside newsagents'
shops for the display of postcards were many pamphlets
and brochures, mostly with bright covers, though some
of these had faded to a toneless yellow that matched the
walls and pillars of the church. The floor was tiled,
orange, green and umber.

Had Charles been visiting this church as a tourist—
and he had never before entered a southern church in
any other spirit—the dingy brilliance that met his eyes
would hardly have struck him, or would at most have
been an amusement. But on his way down from the road,
in his resolution to ask the priest for Christian mercy and
help, his mind had carried him back to the churches
of his childhood and adolescence, the chaste and cold
Lutheran buildings to which his parents had taken him,
the plain stone walls between which he had been con-
firmed, the white clapboard church in which he had
been married. Unconsciously, but certainly, he had expected, after all these years, to re-enter again that clean,
fresh atmosphere, the smell of beeswax and the smoothness of polished chestnut. Instead, he was confronted
with this multi-colored ugliness. And now, not being a
tourist, he failed to notice the lofty and noble propor-
tions of the church itself.

This could not be the temple of the God to whom
he had attempted, and failed, to pray, up there on the
road. Therefore when he found the priest, who was
watching two women arranging flowers in one of the
side chapels, it was the man he saw, not the minister

117

of God. Yet surely this man, just because he was a priest, must help him?

The priest had come to the balustrade which separated the little side chapel from the aisle.

"Father, you must help me. I need your help. I . . ."

He fell silent. The old priest was looking at him neither coldly nor curiously, and the hysteria that Charles had heard in his own voice sounded as false to him as it no doubt did to the priest. The latter said something over his shoulder to the two women, and then, to Charles:

"Follow me."

He led him along the aisle, past the great picture of the Sacred Heart, and through a low door into what Charles assumed to be his vestry. It was a small, bare room. From hooks along one wall hung various vestments. Beneath the single window there stood a table on which were candles and a few papers. There was a shelf with a number of dusty books, and a large, black crucifix. The priest closed the door behind him.

"Father . . ." Charles began at once, and then again fell silent.

"What is it, my son?"

"Father, I am frightened. You must help me. You can save me . . ."

It was not what he had meant to say at all, nor did the voice, cracked and melodramatic, sound like his own. Charles ran his tongue over his lips and did not take his eyes from the lined face of the priest.

"What do you fear, my son?"

With a tremendous effort, Charles managed to make his voice almost normal again. He said:

"Father, do you know what has happened in Siano? Do you know what I have done?"

"Yes, I know."

118

"They're going to kill me, your people. . . . They're waiting to kill me. They won't let me go away. They . . ."

"My son, what are you saying?"

"It's true, you know it's true. Will you help me? Or are you . . . are you on their side?"

The priest raised his hand, a gesture of command, and the noises stopped coming from Charles's lips. It was very quiet in the vestry.

"I am on one side only. That is why I am a priest."

"You don't hate me, do you? I have been foolish, sinful perhaps according to what you think, but you don't hate me, do you?"

"I hate no man. I pity you in your fear and godlessness. I shall pray for you."

And now a thought, which had perhaps been lurking at the back of Charles's mind, came slily to him.

"Father, will you shelter me? Will you take me into your house and let me hide there? I'd be safe in your house. They wouldn't dare, would they . . . ?"

The priest said, slowly and with emphasis:

"I cannot take you into my house. You have seduced a young girl in this village. Why should I shelter her seducer from his own fears? You have broken the law. As a man, I cannot hide you from the law, even should I wish to do so. But you may stay here, in the church, and perhaps if you pray you may make your peace with your God."

Charles spoke bitterly now:

"I see. So that's your religion. If I were a Catholic you'd help me, wouldn't you?" Charles felt immediate shame at the lie he had just spoken. The priest's face had not changed, but he could not stop the words from spilling out of his mouth. "All you want is our souls. You don't care whether I am murdered or not. And you know it was an accident, about the child's death. You know that. But you don't care. You are cruel and wicked."

"My son, think what you are saying. Perhaps the death of the child was an accident. The sins of the flesh are never accidents."

The priest's voice was totally calm and dispassionate. It was a fact that he was stating.

"So you won't help me, you . . . you pharisee."

"I shall pray for you, my son."

"And if they kill me? If you let them kill me?"

"I shall pray for you, my son. And for those men who hate you because you have wronged them. I can do no more. And you, if you can find repentance in your heart . . ."

"You wish me to die, don't you? Say it, say you wish me to die."

"My son, I repeat, I shall pray for you. It is all that I can do. The rest lies with you."

"Have you no . . . ?"

But Charles did not go on. For a long moment he stared into the eyes of the priest. Then he said:

"I am sorry, Father. Will you forgive me for the untrue things that I have said to you?"

"I forgive you, and I shall pray for you."

Slowly Charles turned away. He opened the door that led into the church. No, he could not pray here nor perhaps anywhere else. But the priest had forgiven him. Perhaps if Concetta, too, forgave him. . . . And then he knew that, somehow, he must see her, that she was the key, not only to the past but also to the future, if he were to have a future. Why had he not realized this before, during these days of anguish? He had almost forgotten her, in his own remorse and fear. Yet if

120

she were with him, if she would forgive him and help him. . . . For she had loved him and he, yes, he had loved her. She would save him, he thought as he went out through the doors of the church, she must. The wind in the piazza was dropping.

Chapter Six

BECAUSE, he thought as he walked toward the steps—and now it seemed to him that his mind was completely lucid once again—because, though all else has failed me, my body and the love of my body did not and have not. My wife, my property, my profession, my country, the charity of strangers and the impersonality of power, my will and now my God—it has all been so much smoke when I looked to it for support. But I will not die, this body of mine will not die. It is me, this body, and I am it as I have been now for forty-two years, and that is all I am. And only three days ago this body of mine loved and was loved; that is what will save it, save me, now. That love is the truth and the reality. It is all so very simple. As he reached the beach he glanced up, as for confirmation, to the English tower that floated high upon its headland, golden-yellow in the rays of the afternoon sun.

As a somnambulist is said to walk with unerring sureness along the edges of steep and dangerous places, so Charles climbed the few steps that led to the café terrace. It was deserted, and he pushed through the

121

metal curtain. Up above, on the balcony, the old man had seen him coming and felt a quickening of excitement. Inside the café three fishermen, playing cards, looked up as he came in, but he ignored them. There was no sign of Adelmo, and this Charles recognized at once as being, like the English tower, a proof of his own prescience. Within minutes, seconds even, Concetta would be in his arms, the nightmare passed. He walked straight across the café and through the door at the back. He did not see that one of the fishermen, after a few hurried words with his companions, had got up and left the building.

He went down the short passage and opened both the doors. One led into an empty kitchen, the other into a storeroom where barrels and cases were stacked. Then he climbed the flight of stairs. The first door that he tried was locked.

"Concetta!" he called softly. "Concetta!"

The old man on the balcony had heard him. Quickly he reached for his binoculars and began, with unsteady hands, to search the beach.

Charles took another step along the bare passage. A door opened, and Concetta was standing before him. Her face was drawn and unhappy, her eyes very wide, and he felt a deep pity for her. But now it would be all right.

"Poor child!" he murmured and raised a hand to stroke her cheek.

She drew back into the doorway.

"You're mad to come here . . ."

"I've come for you, Concetta, because I love you."

"You're mad. My father will kill you if he finds you here."

He noted her fear and felt a certain impatience at her

122

slowness in failing immediately to understand why he had come.

"There is no need to be frightened. I love you, and you love me. And therefore . . ."

She had taken a further step away from him, back into her room.

"Go away!" she said. "Please go away!"

He followed her.

"You don't understand, Concetta. I am here because I want to marry you."

"It's too late."

Her eyes were fixed immovably on his.

"Too late? No, no, my darling, it's not too late. I'll get a divorce and marry you . . . I promise."

"Promises. So many promises."

He laughed slightly. It was foolish of her not to grasp what he was saying, but then in his work he often had to explain simple facts to people who could not understand. He spoke gently:

"This is not the time to talk about things that have no importance. All that matters is the love that we have for one another."

Fascinated and frightened by the apparition of this man who seemed so different from her lover, and whom she had been certain she would never see again, she had remained, until this point, almost numb. Now, suddenly, she flushed. She said:

"The other night I waited for you to say it. You didn't. I would have believed you then . . ."

Gently he replied:

"You must believe me now." She shook her head. "I love you, Concetta . . . I love you and I need you . . ."

She looked away, down to the floor.

"You merely need me now."

123

He laid his hand upon her upper arm. And then came the voice from downstairs, a loud, harsh voice, shouting:

"Adelmo! Adelmo!"

The sound tore through the room and Charles felt all his muscles contract. The slow and rainbow-colored world which he had created was splitting asunder. Somehow he must try to recreate it, or at least to hold the fragments together. She was still there, her arm warm beneath his hand. Yet she was shrinking, ceasing to be a certain and protecting goddess. He felt her fear, and now again he felt his own.

"Adelmo! Adelmo!"

There were other voices. His fear was growing with the terrible speed of the shadow cast by a man who has passed by a lamppost on a moonless night. It was engulfing everything.

He pulled her to him and kissed her lips. They did not open, the expression in her eyes did not alter, her body was limp and her hands hung motionless by her sides.

He let her go. He said:

"You won't save me. You don't love me."

She looked at him:

"I did love you . . . until you lied to me. And now, now you are not a man any more. I thought you were a man. Now there is nothing."

The fear was blotting out the world, so that her words came to him as through a mist. The voices were louder, coming up the stairs, and among them he could hear Adelmo's. Charles said:

"Concetta . . ."

She stepped quickly across, closed the door, and turned the key in the lock. Almost at once there was a banging on the door and Adelmo's voice, shouting.

124

"Concetta," said Charles. "Save me."

She pulled him toward the window. A few feet below rose the dunes. As she opened the window a spiral of soft sand blew into the room.

"Quickly . . ." she said.

He stood, his hand in hers and for what seemed a very long time stared into her eyes. The pounding against the door went on.

"Quickly, Carlo . . . Quickly, please, for my sake."

Now, as he had meant to do when first he saw her in the passage, he reached up and stroked her cheek. Then he jumped through the window. Concetta walked across to unlock her door.

It was the old man who first saw him, some twenty yards from the café, running clumsily through the drifting sands.

"*Olà!*" he cried. "*Olà!*"

Then the others were running, too. The old man turned his binoculars from the foreigner, the foul foreigner, to the group of pursuers. Why did they run so slowly? Why did they not hurry and catch him? The old man looked back at the fugitive. He was gaining a little. Soon he would have reached the cliff path that led up to the English tower and the tunnel. Oh, hurry Adelmo, hurry Mario, hurry Antonio, hurry and catch the wicked pagan.

They were shouting as they ran after him, and in the doors and windows of the village faces appeared. Luigi's mother stood on her step and screamed as the foreigner ran by. Up in the post office the postmistress had gone to a window to watch. The mayor could hear the din even in his office and wondered what was happening. Charles ran on.

125

One of the men stopped, picked up a smooth, round stone, and threw it. It caught Charles's shoulder, and the old man saw 'im stumble. But he did not fall. He had reached the bottom of the cliff path.

He was scrambling up it, and the others after him, but now he was clearly gaining on them. Adelmo was no longer in the lead, and the men had to go in single file. Perhaps Antonio did hate this man who had accused him of murdering his own child, but still he should have had the sense to let Mario lead the way. The old man would have liked to shout, to spur them on.

From the steps of the church the priest saw the figures scrambling up the hillside. He crossed himself.

The mayor, from his window, turned about and called. When the *maresciallo* appeared he ordered him to climb the stairs to prevent the criminal from escaping through the tunnel.

The old man lowered his glasses to the pursuers. There were only three of them now. The others had stopped, some at the bottom of the cliff, some a third of the way up. The lazy brutes. He looked higher. The foreigner had reached the top. Now what? If they did not hurry he would reach the tunnel before them. But what was he doing? He was not going toward the tunnel at all! Had the others seen that? Yes, they must have, for they had stopped on the path.

In the round circle of his glasses, the old man tried to distinguish the expression on the foreigner's face. He could not. Quickly he rubbed them on his sleeve, but this was no improvement. The foreigner was walking now, walking slowly at that, and toward the English tower. From all over the village they were watching him, but only the old man could see him clearly. To Maria Spinta, Adelmo, the priest, the mayor, the postmistress, Mario, the old postman, the carabinieri and Concetta he was only a small dark shape who had stopped by the tower. The old man saw him stroke its wall with his hand. The old man saw him look back at Siano. Then, once again, they could all see as he walked slowly toward the edge of the cliff. And what is more, they all knew, at once, what he was seeing.

To his right was the village, and the green dome of the church: to his left the precipitous flank of the mountains: behind him lay the tunnel's dark entrance, which the *maresciallo* had not yet reached: and before him, three hundred feet below, the water was boiling against the rocks and into the caves at the cliff's base. Toward one of these he must go, for there was no fifth way.